LOVE'S PROMISE

LOVE'S MAGIC BOOK 15

BETTY MCLAIN

Copyright (C) 2020 Betty McLain

Layout design and Copyright (C) 2020 by Next Chapter

Published 2020 by Liaison – A Next Chapter Imprint

Edited by Elizabeth N. Love

Cover art by Cover Mint

This book is dedicated to anyone lucky enough to find their own Love's Promise.

CHAPTER 1

Mona Santoes looked around Cut and Curl, the hair salon where she worked. Mona did not have any formal training. She learned everything she knew from her mother, watching her working on ladies' hair. As soon as she was tall enough, her mother let her help. She was giving perms by the time she was eight.

Her dad was gone. He had run out on her mom and Mona when she was two. The only good thing he did was leave them a hundred-acre farm. He signed the deed over to her mom before he left. They were not able to farm it themselves, but they had a place to live, and they leased the land to the McCray ranch. It helped to pay the taxes, so they didn't have to worry about losing their home.

The police brought them news of the death of Mario Santoes two years later. He had died in a car crash. His death had very little impact on their lives. They did not even have to bury him. His girlfriend at the time had already taken care of it for them.

When Mona was eleven, her mom remarried. She married Giles Santoes, a cousin of Mona's dad. They didn't even have to change their last name. Mona soon had two half-sisters and a half-brother. Mona adored the little ones, and they loved her, too. Mona took care of them when she was home from school.

Both Giles and her mom were working the evening shifts. Giles worked as a mechanic at a local garage in Barons. Her mom was working part-time at the Cut and Curl Hair Salon. Everything was going okay for them. They were not wealthy, but they managed to keep food on the table, everyone had decent clothes, and Mona was able to make friends with the girls in her class at school.

After graduation, Mona managed to get Pat, the manager of Cut and Curl, to give her a job doing hair. Giles fixed up an old Chevy car and gave it to Mona for graduation. It provided Mona a way to get back and forth to work.

Mona managed to remain friends with the girls from school. They would come to her to get their hair done. She was happy to be included in the party to Danny's Bar and Grill for Charise's bachelorette party. She very much wanted to look in the magic mirror, but even though she looked more than once, she did not see anyone in the mirror. Mona was disappointed. She was twenty-four, and, after five years working at Cut and Curl, she was beginning to think there was no true love for her.

She was invited to Charise's wedding at the country club. She could not afford a dress fancy enough for a wedding attended by the Governor and a Senator, so she feared she was going to have to make some excuse and turn down the invitation, but Charise solved the problem for Mona when she asked Mona to be one of her bridesmaids. She told the girls not to worry about dresses because Charise was buying all of the bridesmaid dresses, so they would match in the theme she had for the wedding. All they had to do was show up for fittings. Charise also included shoes in the package, so they matched the dresses. Mona was thrilled. She offered to do Charise's makeup and hair for the wedding for free as a wedding gift.

When it came time for Charise to have a new bachelorette party, Zachery flatly refused for it to be at Danny's in Sharpville. Everyone laughed at him, but he was determined, and Charise was so in love with him, she went along with his wishes. The party was held at Fitness Central. The girls told the guys to find another place to be, so the guys went to Danny's.

Charise and Zachery's wedding was scheduled for one week before Christmas. Charise explained to Zachery that school would be out for two weeks for Christmas, so they could have two weeks for a honeymoon, and she would not have to get a sub to teach her fitness class at the school. It also gave them time to make sure their house was ready for them to move into.

Charise and Zachery had made a trip to the military hospital to visit with Dawson Staloc, the Seal Zachery helped to rescue.

"Hi," said Zachery as he and Charise entered the hospital room of Dawson Staloc.

"Hello," greeted Dawson with a big grin as he saw who was there.

"How are you doing?" asked Zachery?"

"I'm very thankful to be alive. I understand I owe my rescue to you, Lieutenant," said Dawson. Zachery looked surprised. Dawson, seeing Zachery's look of surprise, smiled. "Pollack and Fortanos came by to see me. They overheard some guys in the office complaining about your pulling strings when they were there to get their orders. They were glad you had told the ones in charge to give them all of the information instead of sending them in half-prepared."

"I was just looking out for my Seal Team," said Zachery. "This is my fiancée." Zachery pulled Charise forward close to his side.

"Congratulations, Sir," said Dawson. "It's nice to meet you, Ma'am."

"It's nice to meet you, Dawson. I'm glad your rescuers managed to find you and get you home," said Charise.

"So am I, Ma'am," said Dawson.

"Where are you going when you get out of the hospital?" asked Zachery.

"I don't know," said Dawson. "My mom died last year, and my dad and I don't get along. I'll figure something out," said Dawson with a shrug.

Zachery looked at Charise, and she smiled and nodded.

"I'm building an Olympic-size indoor swimming pool. If you want a job, look me up at Fitness Central in Sharpville. I can use a good swimming instructor," said Zachery. "Who better to teach swimming than a Navy Seal?"

Dawson smiled at Zachery. "I will see you as soon as they let me out of here," he said.

"Good," said Zachery. "Take care and follow the doctor's orders, and we will see you soon."

Zachery and Dawson saluted each other, and Charise smiled as she and Zachery left.

They left behind a Seal with new hope for the future.

"Won't he still be a Seal?" asked Charise when they were on their way to the car.

"He will always be a Seal, but he will be an inactive one, for now. After being tortured, his body has to be retrained, and he has to rebuild his stamina. He can not go out on a mission until he is in top shape. He would put the whole team in danger. Being at the swimming pool will be good for him. Swimming is one of the best ways to build stamina and retrain your body," explained Zachery.

"I see," said Charise. "Won't the commanders think you are interfering, again?"

"Probably," agreed Zachery with a grin. "I have to take what pleasure I can."

Charise smiled at him and hugged his arm.

Mona made arrangements to ride to Sharpville with Nessie for the fitting of her bridesmaid dress. They met Evone outside the shop. When they went inside, Stacy, Babs, and Sylvia were already there with Charise.

"Good," said Charise. "We are all here except Gloria. She's away at school. We are the same size, so I can try on her dress."

They all tried on their dresses. Each girl had a different color dress made in the same style. The alterations were set, and the dresses would be ready for pickup in a week. The girls said goodbye outside the shop. Charise was headed for Fitness Central. Babs and Stacy, who had driven in together left for home. Some of the others were going shopping. Nessie asked Mona what she wanted to do. Mona did not hesitate.

"Could we stop at Danny's and get a burger. I would like to look in the magic mirror," said Mona.

Nessie started grinning. "Danny's it is. Maybe if we look often enough, the magic mirror will show us someone just to get rid of us," said Nessie.

Mona laughed. "I am not giving up. I know there is

someone meant just for me. He is waiting for his true love, just like I am. We just need a chance to be together."

"Yeah," agreed Nessie as she parked in front of Danny's, and the girls went in to try to see their future one more time.

There was no one at the mirror, so the girls headed straight for it. Nessie sat down first. She started looking in the magic mirror. A face appeared in the mirror. It looked like someone in a bed looking in a hand mirror. The person in the mirror was being shaved, and he was checking his face. He smiled at the person doing the shaving, and she came into view for a minute. It was a nurse. She left, and the man in the bed looked back in the mirror. He was startled to see Nessie looking at him. He looked around and then back at the mirror.

"Who are you?" he asked.

"I'm Nessie."

"How can I see you?" he asked.

"I am looking in a magic mirror in Danny's in Sharpville," said Nessie. "Who are you?"

"I am Dawson. Do you know Lieutenant Zachery Willis?"

"Yes, he is engaged to a friend of mine," replied Nessie.

"I will be working for him when I get out of the hospital," said Dawson. "I'll see you then. Why does this mirror show us each other?"

"It is a magic mirror. When a girl looks into it, sometimes it will show them their true love," said Nessie.

"You mean you and I are true loves?" asked Dawson.

Nessie shrugged. "The magic mirror seems to think so," she said.

"Well, I'll be," said Dawson. The magic mirror faded back to silver.

Nessie looked up at Mona and smiled. "My true love's

name is Dawson. He is going to be coming here to work for Zachery."

Mona smiled. "I'm so happy for you," she said.

Nessie got up so Mona could sit down.

Mona sat down and looked in the magic mirror. She saw what looked like a reflection of someone looking down into the water. He was turned slightly away and looking to the side. Mona looked at him closely. It looked like Manuel McCray. He looked down at the water and frowned.

"Now, you've moved from my dreams into the daylight," he said. "Why are you haunting me?"

"I am not haunting you," protested Mona.

Manny looked surprised. "You are going to talk to me now," he said.

"I have been seeing you in my dreams for a year now. Always just glimpses of you. If you are real, why haven't you shown yourself before now?" asked Manny.

"I didn't know," protested Mona. "I'm in Danny's looking in the magic mirror. My name is Mona, and you are Manny."

Manny looked startled. "How do you know my name?" he asked.

"I live in Barons," said Mona.

"When can I see you?" asked Manny.

"You need a haircut. Try the Cut and Curl," said Mona.

The image faded before they could say anything else.

Mona looked at Nessie. Nessie had a big smile on her face. "We both have true loves," she said.

"Yes, we do," agreed Mona with satisfaction. "Let's go eat. I'm starved."

They went to a table, and when the waitress came, they ordered burgers. They were very happy with the results of this trip. Both were looking forward to meeting their own true loves.

Manny finished the work he was doing. He headed for the house and went to take a shower. When he was dressed, he went downstairs. His mom, Cathy, and his dad, Alvin, were in the living room. They were sitting on the couch, talking.

Cathy looked at Manny as he came into the room. "Where are you going all dressed up?" she asked.

"I am going to get a haircut," said Manny with a grin.

"A haircut," said Alvin. "You just had one a month ago."

"I need a trim," said Manny. "Do you know where the Cut and Curl is?"

"The Cut and Curl," said Alvin. "What's wrong with Barney's Barber Shop?"

"I thought I would try something different," said Manny.

"The Cut and Curl is behind Molly's Gift Shop," said Cathy.

"Thanks, Mom," said Manny as he started out the door.

"What do you think that was about?" asked Alvin.

"I was wondering," said Cathy. "How many young single girls do you think are working in the Cut and Curl?"

Alvin looked at her and grinned. "So, Manny is interested in a girl working in the Cut and Curl." He frowned. "Why doesn't he just court her? Why does he have to mess with his hair?"

Cathy patted his hand. "Don't worry about it. His hair will grow. I am glad he is showing an interest in someone. We should be in for an interesting time." She grinned at Alvin.

Manny arrived downtown. He went behind Molly's Gift Shop and entered the Cut and Curl. There seemed to be a lot of women in the place. Manny stopped inside the door and looked around.

"Can I help you?" asked the girl at a desk at the entrance.

Manny looked around again. "I want to get a haircut," he said.

"Okay, let me see who is available," she said.

"I want Mona," said Manny.

The girl looked up, startled. Mona didn't have many customers who asked for her by name, and none of them were men. "Mona's on break. Can someone else help you?" she asked.

Manny shook his head. "I want Mona," he said.

Just then, Mona came out of the break room and started to the front. She looked up and saw Manny. He looked at her and started grinning. He had found her, he thought with satisfaction.

Mona smiled. "Manny," she said.

"I came for my haircut," said Manny.

"Come on back," said Mona, leading the way to her station.

Manny followed close behind her. He was giving her the once over as he followed behind her. He grinned. She was nicely put together, he thought.

Mona looked back over her shoulder and grinned when she saw Manny eyeing her figure. Mona motioned for Manny to take a seat, and when he sat down, she put a drape around him.

"Did you have any trouble finding the Cut and Curl?" asked Mona.

"No, my mom told me where it was," said Manny.

Mona put her hand on his face to turn his head and jerked back her hand when she was shocked.

"I'm sorry," she said. Manny had also jumped when he felt the shock. "It must be the magic mirror. Everyone always gets a shock after they see their true love in the magic mirror."

"It's okay. It is not too bad. It just startled me. I wasn't expecting it. I have had worse static electricity shocks," said Manny.

"How am I supposed to cut your hair if I can't touch you?" asked Mona.

Manny took her hand. There was a shock, but it wasn't as bad. It was as if the first shock had drained off some of the power. "See, it's not as bad. Maybe if we keep touching, it will get less," said Manny.

"Maybe," said Mona. She reached for the water bottle to wet his hair. "Do you know how you want it cut?"

"Just a trim," said Manny. "It was getting a little long, and my girl told me I needed a cut." Manny grinned at her.

Mona smiled. "I had to think of a way for us to meet. The magic mirror doesn't give much time for details," she said.

Mona cut his hair silently for a few minutes.

"What did you mean when you said I had been haunting your dreams?" asked Mona.

Manny looked up at her in the mirror in front of him. He could see Mona busy cutting his hair.

"I have been having the same dream for over a year now," said Manny. "I would see you running through this flower garden. I would try to catch you to see you more clearly, but just when I thought I was finally going to catch you, you would disappear."

Mona stopped and stared at him. "Wow." She said. "I wished I had known. I would have stopped and let you catch me."

"I guess fate wasn't ready for us to meet just then," said Manny.

"I guess not," agreed Mona. She ran her fingers through his hair and dusted him off before removing his drape.

Manny stood and looked down at her. "When do you get off?" he asked.

"I was already off when you came in. I stayed so we could talk," said Mona.

"Do you want to go and eat?" asked Manny.

Mona nodded. "Just let me check out, and I'll meet you at the front door."

Mona hurried to check out, and Manny went to pay for the hair cut he hadn't needed. He smiled. It was money well spent, he thought.

CHAPTER 2

The girl at the front desk watched enviously as Mona joined Manny and they left together. They didn't notice. They were too absorbed in each other.

"Is Lou's Diner okay?" asked Manny.

"It's fine," said Mona. "We really don't have much choice if we don't want to drive into Sharpville."

"We can drive to Sharpville if you want to," said Manny.

"No, not tonight, maybe some other time," said Mona. "I've already been to Sharpville today. I don't feel like going back."

"Do you want to drive your car over to Lou's?" asked Manny.

"Yes, I know it is not far and we could walk, but I would like to have my car nearby when we leave," said Mona.

Manny got into his car and followed Mona over to Lou's diner. They parked, and Manny took her hand to go inside. They ignored the slight shock and kept holding hands. When they got inside, Manny led Mona to a booth close to the back. There were not too many people there, and they would be able to talk.

After they ordered their food, Manny looked at Mona and smiled. She smiled back.

"So, you went to Sharpville today," he said.

"Yes," said Mona nodding. "I had a dress fitting. I am going to be a bridesmaid in my friend Charise's wedding," she explained.

Manny shook his head. "Katie told me about the wedding. She said the Governor is going to be there."

"Yes, he is Zachery's Godfather. Senator Willis will be there, too," said Mona. "I wouldn't be going, but Charise is furnishing the bridesmaid's dresses. I'm still a little nervous about it."

Manny squeezed her hand. "You will be the most beautiful girl there." Mona just shook her head and smiled. "You know my last name, but I don't know yours," said Manny.

"It's Santoes; your family leases land from my mom," said Mona.

Manny looked startled. "You mean you have been right next door all of the time?" he asked.

Mona nodded with a grin. "I have seen you at a distance, but we have never had a chance to really meet," said Mona.

Manny grinned. "I guess the magic mirror was ready for us to get together," said Manny.

Mona smiled. "I guess so," she agreed. "I have been looking in the magic mirror a lot. I was beginning to think it was not going to show me anyone," said Mona.

"Maybe I wasn't around any reflective surface," said Manny. "Maybe my dreams were a way to prepare me for the real thing," suggested Manny.

"Maybe, I'm glad you were at the water looking in today," said Mona.

"So am I," agreed Manny with a grin. "I think the magic mirror likes my family. Katie saw Carlos in the magic mirror, and Star saw my brother Sam. They are all very happy."

Manny squeezed her hand, which he was still holding. "When am I going to see you again? Do you have to work tomorrow?"

"No, I am off tomorrow. What about you, I know you stay pretty busy on the ranch?" asked Mona.

"I can ask one of the hands to cover for me. Things are much more relaxed around the ranch since my granddad started hanging out with Sebastian Kantor. He lost all interest in the ranch. It makes things much better for all of us. Would you like to go on a picnic up to the waterfalls?" asked Manny.

"I would love to see the waterfalls. It's beautiful up there," agreed Mona with a smile.

Manny took out his phone. "I need your number so I can reach you if I have any trouble getting away," he said.

Mona gave him the number, and he put the number in his phone. He punched the call button, and Mona's phone rang. Manny smiled as she looked at her screen. "Now you have my number, in case you need to call me," he said.

Mona saved the number to her phone under Manny's name. She smiled as she put her phone away. "What are you going to be doing during Christmas break?" she asked.

Manny shrugged. "I haven't made any plans. I imagine Mom will try to get everyone out to the ranch for Christmas," he said.

"Charise and Zachery are getting married a week before Christmas at the country club. I know Katie and Carlos will be there. Sam and Star will probably be there, also. Would you like to go as my date? I have to march down the aisle at the ceremony, but the rest of the time, we could dance and eat and enjoy ourselves. We may even get to say hello to Senator Willis and Governor Hayes."

Manny paused. He wasn't used to going to fancy parties. "Would I have to wear a tux?" he asked.

Mona shook her head. "A suit will do. The only ones wearing a tux will be the groom and best man. The rest of the guys will be wearing suits."

"I would love to go with you," said Manny. "I would love to hold you in my arms and dance. Besides, I want all of the guys to know you are taken. You are mine. They need to keep looking."

Mona smiled. "I don't think you have to worry about other guys. They haven't exactly been beating a path to my door."

"I'm glad the guys around here are so blind. I'm glad you were saved for me," said Manny.

"We need to go," said Mona. "I think they are about ready to close."

They went to the front where Manny paid for their food. After paying, they went outside where they lingered beside Mona's car. They were both reluctant to say good night. They stood looking in each other's eyes until Manny leaned down and gently kissed her.

Mona sighed and leaned in and laid her head against his chest. Manny put his arms around her and held her for a minute. Mona pulled back and looked into his face. "I guess I should go," she whispered.

"I guess," said Manny. He kissed her again. "I will follow you home."

Mona smiled. "You don't have to follow me. It's not too far."

"I'll follow," insisted Manny.

"Okay," agreed Mona getting in her car.

Manny entered his car and waited for Mona to pull out, then followed her home. It was about a ten-minute drive, not far from the McCray ranch. Manny parked behind Mona and got out of his car. He went up and opened Mona's door for her and helped her out. As soon as she was standing, Manny held her close and kissed her again.

"I'll see you in the morning about nine," he said.

"I'll be waiting," agreed Mona.

She watched as Manny turned and entered his car. He backed up and turned. Manny waved as he started to leave. Mona waved back. With a sigh, she turned and started for the door. Her ten-year-old brother Glen opened the door.

"Hi, Mona," he said

"Hi, Squirt," said Mona bending down and hugging him.

"Who was in the car behind you?" asked Glen.

"It was Manny McCray from the ranch," said Mona.

"Do you like him?" asked Glen.

"Yes, I do, why?" asked Mona.

"I was just wondering," said Glen.

Mona took his hand and started toward the kitchen. "Have you eaten?" asked Mona.

"No, Mom's lying down with a headache, and Beth and Poppie are in their rooms doing homework," he replied.

Mona frowned. She doubted they were doing homework. She was going to have to talk to them about making sure Glen had something to eat.

"What do you want to eat?" asked Mona.

"Mac and cheese," said Glen with a grin.

Mona ruffled his hair. "I should have known. You would live on mac and cheese if you could," she laughed.

"I like it," agreed Glen with a smile.

Mona put his mac and cheese on to cook and then looked to see what else they had to go with it. She opened a can of beans and put it in a boiler. She cut up some wieners and stirred them into the beans. She pulled out a can of rolls and put them into the oven to bake. She poured Glen a glass of milk and sat him down at the table while she stirred the mac and cheese.

"Have you done your homework?" asked Mona.

Glen nodded. "I did it as soon as I came home from school," said Glen. "I have some papers the teacher wants signed. I have to take them back tomorrow."

"I'll sign them after you eat," said Mona.

Mona always signed their papers and made sure their homework was done. Their mom, Jewel, was always having headaches. Mona had urged her to go to the doctor and find out their cause, but so far, she had not been able to convince her to go.

Mona stirred the mac and cheese and put some on a plate for Glen. She added some of the beans and wieners. After putting a roll on his plate, she set it in front of Glen and smiled as she watched him dig in.

Beth and Poppie had smelled the food and emerged from their rooms. They both came and filled plates for themselves and sat at the table to eat.

"Have you two finished your homework?" she asked.

"I'm finished," said Poppie.

"I'm almost done," said Beth.

"Well, you can finish as soon as you clean the kitchen," said Mona.

Beth looked like she wanted to protest, but she changed her mind and was silent.

"I want to see your schoolwork as soon as you are finished," said Mona. "I'll look over Glen's while you are cleaning the kitchen."

"Can I take my lunch tomorrow, Mona?" asked Glen.

"Why do you want to take your lunch instead of eating in the lunchroom?" asked Mona.

Glen hung his head and didn't look at Mona.

"Glen, what's wrong?" asked Mona.

"Some of the kids were teasing me because I get a free lunch," said Glen.

Mona pursed her lips. She had gone through the same thing when she had been in school. She had solved the problem by taking her lunch, too. She was not going to let Glen suffer. She needed to go and talk to the principal and teachers. "You can take your lunch tomorrow," said Mona to Glen, who had been looking anxious.

Glen relaxed and smiled. "Thanks, Mona," he said.

The next morning, Mona fixed Glen a lunch to take to school with him. After the school bus left, Mona hurried to be ready for Manny's arrival.

When she came into the living room, her mom was there lying on the sofa. Mona stopped and looked at her. She didn't look well. "Are you feeling better?" asked Mona.

Jewel looked at Mona without answering her. "Are you going somewhere?" she asked.

"Yes, I am. I am going on a picnic with Manny McCray," said Mona.

"Is he the one Hazel was telling about him coming into the Cut and Curl to get a haircut? She said he would not let anyone cut his hair but you."

"Yes, he is," said Mona. "He didn't really need a haircut. He came in to see me."

"I see," said Jewel. "I hope you know what you are doing."

"I am very aware of what I am doing. I am going on a picnic with a great guy. One who treats me with respect, can't you be happy for me?"

Jewel sighed and lay back and closed her eyes.

There was a knock at the door. Mona went to open it. She smiled back at Manny as he smiled at her. "Are you ready?" he asked.

Mona nodded. She turned and called out to her mom, "I'll be here when the school bus comes." There was no answer, so Mona went out and closed the door behind her.

When they were in the car, Mona looked at Manny and smiled.

"Could we make a stop at the school on the way? Some boys have been bullying my brother Glen, and I need to see if I can get it stopped," said Mona.

"Sure, we can stop. How old is Glen?" asked Manny.

"He is ten. He is in the fifth grade. He asked me last night if he could bring his lunch from home. The boys are picking on him because he gets a free lunch. I made him a lunch. I didn't have the heart to tell him they probably wouldn't stop. I thought I would talk to the principal and his teacher," said Mona.

Manny pulled to a stop in the school parking lot. He got out and came around and opened her door.

"You don't have to come in with me," said Mona.

"I want to if you have no objection. I may know the boys. We had a problem with them on the ranch. If it is them, their fathers work for me. I warned them if I caught them bullying anyone else, I would take care of them," said Manny. "I need to know if it is them."

"Okay," said Mona as she took his hand and headed for the school office.

The secretary smiled at them when they entered. "May I help you?" she asked.

"Yes, I would like to see Principal Webb," said Mona.

"Have a seat. I'll go and get him," she said.

They sat in the chairs by the wall, and the secretary went into the principal's office.

She was back in just a minute with Principal Webb following her.

The principal came forward and smiled at them. "Hello, Mona. Hello, Manny. Come into my office so we can talk," he said. They rose and followed him into his office. "Have a seat," he said as he closed the office door. He went behind his desk and sat down. "Now, what can I help you with?"

"I wanted to talk to you about my brother, Glen," said Mona.

"Fifth grade, right," said Principal Webb.

"Yes," agreed Mona. "Glen is being bullied by some boys because he is getting a free lunch. I thought if I bought him a lunch card, it might help."

Principal Webb shook his head. "I should have fixed it where the children getting a free lunch would not be singled out. You do not have to buy him a lunch card. I can make him a card. It will be free, but no one else will know it is free but me. I'll put my code on the card so I can tell which ones to charge the state for." He took out a card and filled it out and stamped it. "It will look just like everyone else's card," said Principal Webb. He handed the card to Mona.

She looked it over and smiled. "May I take it to his room and give it to him?" asked Mona.

"Sure, it was nice to see you both. If Glen has any more problems, let me know," he said.

They said goodbye and left his office and headed for Glen's schoolroom.

Mona tapped on the door and waited for a "come in" before opening the door. She and Manny went over to the teacher's desk.

"I'm sorry to disturb class, Mrs. Perry," said Mona. "Glen left his lunch card home, and I brought it for him."

Manny had been looking around the class. He spotted the two boys and gave them a hard look.

"Glen, you may come and take your lunch card," said

Mrs. Perry. Glen came up and took the card. He smiled at Mona and went back to his seat.

"Thank you, Mrs. Perry," said Mona.

"Mrs. Perry," said Manny. "Would it be alright for me to tell Jimmy and Steve to meet me in my office as soon as they arrive home from school?"

"Of course, did you boys understand?" asked Mrs. Perry.

Both boys nodded their heads and looked away. Manny nodded his head, and, taking Mona's hand, they left to go on their picnic.

CHAPTER 3

*M*anny picked a spot close to the waterfalls to have their picnic. They got out of the car, and Mona stood gazing at the falls as Manny went to the back of his car to get the blanket and a large picnic basket.

Mona went over to help him spread the blanket for them to sit on. After the blanket was spread, Manny sat the basket in the center of it.

"Wow, that's a big basket. Did you fix it?" asked Mona.

"No, I called Lou's and had it prepared for me. I went in to pick it up before I came to your house," said Manny.

"I could have fixed us a lunch," protested Mona.

"I know, but I wanted you to relax and enjoy yourself," said Manny. "Do you want to eat first or explore first?" asked Manny.

"Eat first. Then, we can clean up and put everything in the car instead of leaving it out to attract animals," said Mona.

"Okay," agreed Manny. He opened the basket to see what was there.

He pulled out a bowl of mashed potatoes. Next was a salad. There was also fried chicken. There was a large container of iced tea and glasses. Last was two large slices of chocolate cake. There were paper plates and plastic utensils.

Mona opened the containers and started making plates for each of them. She handed Manny a plate. He closed the picnic basket, and they used the top for a table. They were sitting on the blanket on either side of the picnic basket.

"This is good," said Mona, taking a bite of the salad. She picked up a piece of chicken and started eating it. Manny reached for a piece and started eating his piece.

"You and Glen seemed close," said Manny.

"Yeah, I was close to Beth and Poppie, but it seems the older they get, the more they pull away from me," said Mona with a sigh.

"Most kids do as they grow up," said Manny.

"I guess," said Mona with a sigh. "Are you close with your brothers and Katie?" asked Mona.

"We are getting closer. Our granddad tried to drive a wedge between us, but since he started hanging out with Sebastian Kantor, he has lost all interest in us and the ranch. It makes it much better for all of us," said Manny.

"I heard some things about your granddad and Sebastian Kantor at Cut and Curl. He is a favorite topic of conversation for the people around here."

Manny grinned. "I imagine it is a lot like the barbershop. If you sit and listen, they will tell you everything happening in the area," said Manny.

Mona smiled. "Pretty much, if someone doesn't talk about it, it is not worth knowing. I imagine we are their favorite topic of conversation today."

"You think so?" asked Manny grinning.

Mona nodded. "The woman at the sign-in has already called Mom and told her about your visit to get a haircut," said Mona.

Manny shook his head. "It must be a slow news day."

Mona laughed. "A good-looking guy comes in asking for me is news around Barons."

Manny pulled the chocolate cake out and opened one slice. He dipped his fork in and offered Mona a bite. She opened her mouth, and he slid the cake inside.

"Ummmm," said Mona. "It's so good," she said.

Manny smiled as he offered her another bite before taking a bite for himself. "It is good," said Manny. "I'm going to have to remember to order it next time I go to Lou's." They finished off the cake and started putting everything back in the basket and folding up the blanket. Manny carried the basket, and Mona carried the blanket to be put in the trunk of the car.

"Are you ready for our walk?" asked Manny, reaching for her hand and ignoring the shock.

Mona smiled and squeezed his hand. "I need to walk after all of that cake," she said as they started walking toward the waterfalls. There was a path around the falls. They started following it around to the top. Mona tried to watch where she was walking and see everything around her at the same time. She held onto Manny's hand. She was enjoying the feeling of being close to him. Manny seemed to be experiencing the same feelings. He held her hand and stayed close to her side and smiled down at her often as he guided her to the top of the falls. They stopped at the top and gazed around.

Manny put his arm around Mona and pulled her close to his side as they watched the power of the water as it went over the falls. "It's magnificent," said Mona.

"Yes," agreed Manny, watching the look on Mona's face as she gazed at the falls. "It is indeed beautiful."

Mona looked up at Manny and smiled. "Thank you for bringing me here. I haven't been here in years. I had forgotten how wonderful it is."

"Somehow, it seems even more beautiful today, with you by my side," said Manny.

They turned after a few more minutes and started back around. After they had gone a ways, Mona sighed. "The falls is beautiful, but it is nice to put a little distance between us and the noise," she said.

Manny laughed. "It is the only drawback," he agreed.

When they arrived back at the car, Manny stopped before opening Mona's door and turned her toward him. He pulled her close and kissed her.

"Thank you for coming with me today," he said as he kissed her again.

"Thank you for asking me. I had a great time, and you can tell Lou the food was wonderful, especially the cake," said Mona, raising her face for another kiss. Manny was happy to oblige her.

After a few more kisses, they stopped and rested while catching their breath. Manny opened the door and helped Mona into the car. "When am I going to see you again?" asked Manny.

"We could go somewhere tomorrow after work," said Mona.

"We could drive into Sharpville and see a movie," suggested Manny.

"I don't care what we do as long as I can be close to you," declared Mona.

Manny smiled at her. "I'll see you after work. What time do you finish?" he asked.

"My shift ends at three-thirty," she said.

"I'll pick you up at your house at four," said Manny.

"Okay," agreed Mona.

Manny pulled to a stop behind Mona's car and went around to open her door. He walked her to the house and kissed her before turning to leave. Manny turned his car and waved at Mona as she stood watching him leave. She waved back and went inside. Mona looked at the sofa, but it was empty.

Mona went toward the kitchen. She wanted to prepare a meal and have it ready when the school bus ran.

When the bus ran, Glen, Poppie, and Beth hurried inside. They headed for the kitchen when they smelled food. Mona had the table set and the food on the table.

When Glen came into the kitchen, he ran and hugged Mona. Mona hugged him back and waited for a minute before saying anything. "Thank you for bringing me a lunch card," said Glen.

"Did the boys bother you anymore?" asked Mona.

Glen shook his head with a big smile. "They never said a word to me after you came. I saw them talking to each other, but they did not talk to me."

"Good, if they start bothering you again, you let me know," said Mona.

"Now, all of you wash your hands so you can eat." The girls had been about to sit down. They quickly turned to go wash their hands.

Glen looked up at Mona and smiled. "You will tell Mr. McCray thank you for coming to the school?" asked Glen.

"I already thanked him, but I will be sure and tell him you said thanks. Now go wash up so you can eat," said Mona.

Glen hurried away to wash his hands.

Meanwhile, at the McCray ranch, Manny looked up from his work in his office to find Jimmy and Steve standing in his doorway.

"Come in," said Manny. "Have a seat. We'll have a talk as soon as your dads get here."

The boys looked toward the door as first Jimmy's dad and then Steve's dad came in. They stood back and waited to see what Manny wanted with them. He had not told them anything except to come to the office.

Manny stared hard at the boys. "What did I tell you about bullying other children?" he asked.

"You told us not to do it," said Steve.

"What did I tell you would happen if I found out you were doing it again?" asked Manny.

"You told us you would take care of us," said Jimmy.

"Were you under the impression I meant something good?" asked Manny.

"No, Sir," answered both boys.

"Then why were you bullying Glen Santoes?" asked Glen. The boys looked at each other and then back at Manny. "He didn't tell me. I figured it out on my own, and you just confirmed it for me. Now, what do you think your punishment should be?" asked Manny. "I won't have bullies on my ranch. I could fire your dads and have you all moved from the ranch," said Manny.

Both dads looked startled at this observation. Manny ignored them; he was concentrating on the boys. Both boys looked like they were about to cry. They never dreamed they could lose their home over what they had been doing "We are sorry. We won't ever do it again," said Jimmy.

"You told me the same thing the last time, yet here you are again doing the same thing," said Manny.

"We will take any punishment you say, but please don't fire our dads. It's not their fault," said Steve.

Manny looked at them hard for a few minutes. "I want you both in the stables as soon as you get home from school and on Saturday. You will clean the stalls and put out fresh hay and feed for the horses. You will work three hours each day and seven hours on Saturday. I don't want to hear any complaining from either of you. You will keep to the job for a month. I will be checking to be sure you do a good job, and if I hear of any more bullying, I won't be so easy on you. Do you understand?" asked Manny.

"Yes, Sir," said both boys.

"Since it is late today, you only have to put out hay and feed today. I will expect to see you both tomorrow as soon as the bus runs. Any time I am not here, your dads will let me know if you don't do your job. You can go now," said Manny.

The boys scrambled out of their chairs and hurried to get started. Manny waited until the boys were gone before looking at their dads. "I'm sorry I had to threaten your jobs," he said. "I wanted to impress on the boys just how serious their behavior was."

Jimmy's dad looked at Manny. "We understand. Our talking to them hasn't done any good. I hope you got through to them."

"Let me know if you have any problems with them. I won't be here tomorrow night. I have a date," said Manny with a grin.

Both guys grinned at him. "They will never know you aren't here. We will cover for you," said Steve's dad.

"Thanks. Now, you two get back to work and don't look so happy. We don't want the boys to get the wrong impression."

"Yes, Sir, Boss," they said, leaving after putting a serious expression on their faces.

Manny left his office and went to the house. His mom and dad were in the dining room, sitting at the table. His mom had dinner cooking and was keeping an eye on it while she talked to his dad.

"Hi," said Manny, kissing his mom's cheek and going around the table to talk to his dad.

"I have Steve and Jimmy working in the stables for the next month. They will be there three hours each day after school and seven hours on Saturday. They are being taught a lesson, so don't let them go early. If they ask you anything, tell them to check with me," said Manny.

"What did they do?" asked Cathy.

"They were bullying Glen Santoes. I found out about it and called them on it. They have accepted their punishment. I told them if it happened again, I would have to fire their dads and they would have to move. I hope I got through to them. I think they are good boys. They just need something to do and something to keep them from being bored," said Manny.

"Well, you took care of it. I don't think they are going to be bored for the next month," said Alvin with a grin.

"What are their dads going to say when they find out you put the boys to work?" asked Cathy.

"They already know. They were in the office when I talked with the boys. They were all for it. They said they had been trying to talk to the boys but were getting nowhere. They are hoping this works," said Manny.

"If Granddad shows up, try to keep him away from the boys. I don't want him to confuse them," said Manny. "I need to warn David, too. He needs to know what's going on."

"I'll let him know," said Alvin. "I'll be working fence line with him tomorrow."

"I'll be leaving early tomorrow. I have a date. We will be going to a movie in Sharpville," said Manny.

"Oh, okay," said Cathy. "Are you going to tell us who she is?"

"I am seeing Mona Santoes. She saw me in the magic mirror."

"Well," said Cathy. "The magic mirror sure likes our family. I wonder who it has picked out for Thomas."

Alvin and Manny burst out laughing. "I guess we will just have to wait and see," said Alvin with a big grin.

"You are going to have to invite Mona over for supper soon," said Cathy.

"I will soon, but it may have to wait until after Charise's wedding. Mona is in the wedding party, and I am going as her guest," said Manny with a grin at his mom.

"You're going to meet Governor Hayes! You need a new suit," declared Cathy.

Manny laughed. "I have several very nice suits," said Manny.

"You have to get a new suit," stated Cathy.

"No need to argue. You may as well give in," said Alvin. "You know your mom will just keep on until you give in."

"Okay, Mom, I will get a new suit," said Manny, grinning at his mom.

"Good, I can't have my son meeting the governor in an old suit," said Cathy.

Manny shook his head and went to take a shower and call Mona.

CHAPTER 4

*A*fter Manny finished his shower, he lay back against his pillows at the head of his bead and called Mona.

"Hello," answered Mona.

"Hi," said Manny.

"Manny," said Mona.

"I miss you," said Manny.

"I miss you, too. Tomorrow can't come soon enough," said Mona.

"I just want to hold you in my arms and feel your heart beating along with mine. Just knowing we are meant to be one is making my heart beat faster. I want to smother you with kisses and know you are as happy to be in my arms as I am to have you there," Manny spoke softly.

"Whew," said Mona. "If this keeps up, I will have to turn on the fan." She turned serious after her remark. "Every word you are saying makes me feel loved, and I want the same thing. Ever since I saw you in the magic mirror, all I have wanted is to be close to you. Every minute I spend with you I savor, and every minute away from you I am waiting until I can be with you again. You are my light in the darkness. With you by my side I know I will experience all of life's joys because we are meant to be with each other," said Mona.

"I know it is not manly, but your words make me want to cry. They are so beautiful. I feel the same way. How am I supposed to sleep when all I want to do is jump in my car and drive to your side?" asked Manny.

Mona smiled. "At least you shouldn't be having any more of those dreams. If one pops up, stop and say, 'Mona, wait for me,' Then we can be together in dreams as well as real life."

"I am past the dreams. The real you is much better," said Manny.

"Did you know, some of my friends say they can mind talk to the guys they have seen in the magic mirror," said Mona.

"What's mind talk?" asked Manny.

"It's where you close your eyes and think what you want to say and your true love can hear your thoughts," said Mona.

"Wow, does it work?" asked Manny.

"I don't know. Do you want to try?" asked Mona.

"Yes, what do I do?" asked Manny.

"I love you," thought Mona

"I love you, too," thought Manny.

"It works," thought Mona.

"I love it. I can have a conversation with you, and no one can hear. If I am not around a phone, I can still talk to you. This is great. I love it, and I love you," thought Manny.

Mona laughed. "Do you want to hang up the phone and have mind talk?" asked Mona.

"I need to let you get some sleep so you won't fall asleep during the movie tomorrow," said Manny.

"Alright, before you hang up, Glen asked me to thank you for helping out with his problem at school. He made me promise to tell you he said thanks," said Mona.

"Tell him I was glad to help and if he has any more problems to let me know," said Manny.

"I will. Good night I'll see you tomorrow," said Mona. They hung up the phones.

"Good night I love you," thought Manny.

"Good night. I love you, too," thought Mona.

Mona turned her face into the pillow and held it tight. She was so happy. Life was so good. She finally drifted off to sleep. In her dreams, Manny was there. He was holding her close and protecting her. She felt so safe and loved.

Manny had drifted off to sleep, also. In his dreams, Mona was there. He was holding her close and keeping her safe. The love they shared wrapped around them and enfolded them together.

The next morning both Manny and Mona awoke refreshed from a very good night's sleep. They both were excited about the day to come and seeing each other again.

Manny was in a great mood the next morning. His mom smiled as she watched him eat his breakfast. She was so glad things were working out for Manny. He deserved the very best. Cathy smiled and looked in the mirror in the dining room.

"Hmmm, I think I'll see about doing my hair. I wonder if I can get an appointment at the Cut and Curl," thought Cathy. She called and made an appointment for a wash and set and asked for Mona.

When she hung up the phone, Cathy rubbed her hands in satisfaction. There was more than one way to go about meeting someone. After she cleared the breakfast things away and left a note for Alvin, saying she was going to town shopping, Cathy headed for Barons. She did her shopping first while waiting for the time of her appointment. Then, she headed for the Cut and Curl.

When Cathy entered the Cut and Curl, the lady at the entrance desk looked up at her and smiled.

"Can I help you?" she asked.

"I have an appointment for a wash and set. My name is Cathy McCray."

"Yes, Mrs. McCray, if you will have a seat, Mona will be right with you," she said.

"Thank you," said Cathy taking a seat to wait.

Mona came forward, showing her client to the front after fixing her hair. After the lady had paid and left, Mona smiled at Cathy. "If you will follow me," she said.

Cathy rose and followed Mona back to her station.

"How are you, today, Mrs. McCray?" asked Mona.

"I'm fine. Do you know who I am?" asked Cathy.

"Yes," nodded Mona. "I know you are Manny's mother. It's very nice to meet you. I've seen you around, but we have never met."

"I hope you don't mind my coming in like this. I get so impatient waiting for others to make up their minds to get together," said Cathy.

Mona laughed. "I don't mind at all. I wanted to meet you and your husband, too. I didn't want to push Manny before he was ready," said Mona. She had put the drape around Cathy's shoulders and fastened it. "If you will come with me to the back, we can shampoo your hair."

Cathy rose and followed her to the back and sat in another chair. Mona raised the chair and tilted it back so she could shampoo Cathy's hair.

"You have lovely hair," said Mona. "How do you want it styled?" asked Mona.

"Thank you," said Cathy. "I like the style I had. It will be fine."

"Okay," agreed Mona.

She helped Cathy up and dried her hair. They went back to Mona's station. Mona rubbed a styling gel into Cathy's hair and massaged it in well. She then picked out rollers and started rolling Cathy's hair.

They talked while Mona was putting in the rollers. They were getting to know each other. Cathy was impressed with how well-spoken Mona was, and she liked the way Mona's face would light up whenever Manny's name was mentioned.

Mona found Cathy easy to talk to, and she enjoyed hearing about Manny at a younger age.

When the rollers were done, Mona led Cathy over and sat her under a dryer. The dryer was too loud for them to talk, so she gave her a magazine to look at while her hair was drying. Mona went to her station and cleaned around it while she waited for Cathy's hair to dry.

After about twenty minutes, Mona went over and checked Cathy's hair to see if it was ready. She decided it was ready, so she led the way back to her station.

"I'm glad you came in today so we could meet." said Mona as she took the rollers out of Cathy's hair.

"I am, too," said Cathy. "I understand you are going to be in Charise's wedding party."

"Yes, I am. I asked Manny to be my escort. I didn't want to spend an evening around all those people without Manny," said Mona.

She was working on Cathy's hair. She would style it and then spray it, then she would style some more. When she had it styled, Mona held a towel in front of Cathy's face and sprayed it again. After she was done, Mona waved the towel around to get rid of the fumes. Then, she turned Cathy around and let her look in the mirror.

"Oh my, it's the same but different. It looks so alive," said Cathy.

Mona smiled. "I'm glad you like it," she said.

"I love it," said Cathy. "Do I pay up front?"

"It's on the house," said Mona.

"Oh no, I didn't mean for you to do my hair for free," said Cathy.

"I want to, after all, I can do my future mother-in-law's hair for free if I want to," said Mona.

Cathy hugged her. "I am so glad the magic mirror picked you for my son," she said.

"So am I," agreed Mona. She walked Cathy to the door and bid her goodbye.

"Your last client didn't pay," said Hazel from the front desk.

"Put it on my tab, and don't forget to give me my employee discount," said Mona.

"She's not an employee."

"I am," said Mona, "and she is my future mother-in-law."

Hazel made a note about Mrs. McCray's appointment and the charges and looked at Mona. "You and Manny are really together."

Mona smiled. "Yes, we really are," she agreed.

Mona left to go and finish straightening her station. It was time for her lunch break. Mona decided to go to Lou's for lunch. She usually brought her lunch and ate in the small park in downtown Barons, but today she felt like splurging.

When Mona went in, she spotted Babs in a booth at the back. Babs motioned for Mona to join her, so Mona took her food and went to join Babs.

"Hi," said Mona. "I haven't seen you lately. How are you and Wilson doing?"

Babs smiled. "We are doing great. Wilson is really enjoying working at the fire station. Captain Donaldson is teaching him all he needs to know about running the fire station. He wants to be sure Wilson is ready to take over, so he can retire. Wilson is starting something new at the fire station. Once a month they are going to have a movie night. They have a large-screen TV mounted on the wall. They have a couple of sofas and a table with eight chairs. They have a sleeping place upstairs, but sometimes one or two of the guys will sleep on the sofas. Well, Wilson is letting them invite their wives or girlfriends in for a movie night. They will have three or four movies to pick from and they can all watch the movie and visit. The ladies will bring finger food and chips with dips, and the guys will furnish a cooler with ice and sodas. No alcohol, it's not allowed in the fire station. Everything will be fine as long as they don't get a fire alarm."

"It sounds like a great idea," said Mona.

"Yes, would you and Manny like to join us tonight?" asked Babs. "Captain Donaldson's wife will be there along with his two boys. Sylvia and Henry are joining us, and Stacy and Jason are going to be there."

"What time does it start?" asked Mona.

"We are going to start at five," said Babs.

"What food should I bring?" asked Mona.

"Whatever you want, just as long as it can be eaten with your fingers. We have paper plates but no utensils," said Babs.

"I'll check with Manny and, if he can't make it, I will let you know. If I don't call, we will be there," said Mona. Both girls took their trash to throw away and headed back to work.

When Mona was back at her workstation, while she was waiting for her next client, she sat in her chair and leaned back and thought of Manny. "Manny, are you there?" she thought.

"Yes, is something wrong?"

"No, I just talked to Babs at lunch. They are having movie

night at the local fire station tonight. She invited us. Do you want to go and meet some of my friends?" thought Mona.

"What time does it start?" thought Manny.

"It starts at five," thought Mona.

"Do we need to bring anything?" thought Manny.

"Something to snack on; Babs called it finger food."

"How about popcorn?" thought Manny.

"Popcorn would be great. What is a movie without popcorn?" thought Mona.

"Mom has a bunch of paper bags to put popcorn in. If you will pop the corn, I will bring the bags, and we can fill them to take with us," thought Manny.

"Okay, I'll pick up some popcorn after work and pop it as soon as I get home. Are you still going to be at my house at four?" thought Mona.

"Yes, I can help you make the popcorn and bag it. I will bring a box to carry the bags in, so they don't spill," thought Manny.

"I will see you then. I have to get to work. I love you," thought Mona.

"I love you, too," thought Manny.

Mona sat up straight, then rose to greet her next client. Smiling was no problem. She was very happy.

Manny sat at his desk, smiling and thinking about Mona. He looked up as Alvin entered his office. Alvin looked at his son's smiling face and then went over and sat in the chair in front of the desk.

"I told David about the boys," said Alvin.

"Good," said Manny absently.

"Your mom went to town today. She stopped in at the Cut and Curl and had her hair done," said Alvin.

Manny's head came up fast. "What!"

"Take it easy. She just wanted to meet and say hello to

Mona," said Alvin. "Apparently, they got along fine. Your mom loves her hair, and she has all good things to say about Mona."

"I was just talking to Mona. She didn't say anything about it," said Manny.

"She probably wanted to wait and tell you in person," said Alvin.

Manny shrugged. "Maybe, we were busy talking about tonight. We really didn't talk about anything else," said Manny.

"What's happening tonight?" asked Alvin.

"Movie night at the fire station," said Manny with a grin.

Alvin laughed. "Times sure have changed. Let's hope there are no fire alarms tonight," said Alvin.

"Things have changed a lot for me since I met Mona," said Manny. "I'm glad the old man has found peace and is letting the rest of us enjoy our lives," said Alvin.

"Me, too," agreed Manny. "I need to send Katie a huge bouquet of roses to thank her for straightening everything out with the old man."

"She would like that," agreed Alvin.

Alvin rose and headed for the door. "I'll let you get back to work."

"Tell Mom I need some popcorn bags. Mona and I are going to popcorn to take for movie night," said Manny.

Alvin grinned. "I'll tell her," he said as he left. Alvin went to the house and delivered his message.

"He wasn't upset about me going in to see Mona, was he?" she asked.

Alvin smiled as he drew her close and kissed her. "No, he was startled, but I think he was pleased the two of you got along so well," said Alvin.

"She's a lovely girl," said Cathy. "She's perfect for Manny.

I am glad the magic mirror thought so, too." Alvin hugged her one more time and then went back out to work.

Manny took off work a little early so he could take a shower and change before going to Mona's. He collected the popcorn bags and left for the farm next door.

Mona was pulling into the front of her house when Manny drove up. She waited beside her car for him to park and join her. When he reached her side, he sat the box he was carrying on top of her car and drew her into his arms. She raised her face for a kiss.

When they came up for air, Manny still held her close. "I have been dreaming of kissing you all day," said Manny.

"I always wanted to be a dream come true," said Mona with a smile.

Manny chuckled. "You are definitely my dream come true," he said.

"You are all of my dreams come true," whispered Mona.

After one more kiss, Manny drew back. "Are you ready to pop some corn?" he asked.

Mona laughed. "I will have to be sure and not eat too much of it while I am making it. I love popcorn," said Mona.

Manny collected his box from the top of the car, and they headed inside.

CHAPTER 5

They found Glen in the dining room when they went inside. He was doing his homework.

"Hi, Glen," said Mona, giving him a hug.

"Hi. Hello, Mr. McCray," said Glen.

"Hello, Glen," said Manny.

"Are the girls in their rooms?" asked Mona.

"Yes, they don't like being in here," said Glen.

Mona looked at Glen and frowned. She didn't like him being by himself so much. She was worried about him.

"Did you have something to eat?" she asked.

"I made me a sandwich," said Glen.

Manny could see Mona was bothered about Glen being by himself. "Didn't you say Captain Donaldson was going to have his boys there tonight?" asked Manny.

"Yes, he is," said Mona, looking at Manny while she got out the corn popper.

"If Glen has his homework finished, why can't he come with us? He could play with Donaldson's boys or watch the movie," said Manny.

"You wouldn't mind?" asked Mona.

Manny put his arm around her. "It was my idea," he said.

Mona looked at Glen. "We are going to a movie night at the fire station tonight. Would you like to go with us?" she asked.

Glen's face lighted up. "Will it be alright with Dad and Mom?" he asked.

"They won't care as long as you don't stay out too late," assured Mona. "Do you want to come with us?"

"Yes," said Glen, nodding his head.

"Thanks, Mr. McCray," he said.

"You are welcome. Why don't you call me Manny? There is lots of Mr. McCrays around. It could get confusing," said Manny.

"Okay," agreed Glen.

The first pan of popcorn finished. Mona started filling bags. Manny came over and started helping.

"Why don't you start the next popper? I'll take care of this," said Manny.

"Okay," agreed Mona.

They worked well together while Glen sat at the table and watched as he finished his homework. They were soon done, and Manny loaded all of the bags into the box to take to the fire station.

When they were ready to go, Mona went to her mom's room and told her she was taking Glen with her. Her mom didn't say anything, so Mona went to Beth's room and told her in case Giles came home before they returned and wanted to know where Glen was. Mona shook her head as she went downstairs. She was going to have to make sure Glen didn't spend too much time by himself.

When Mona returned to the living room, she found Manny and Glen waiting for her. Manny had even convinced Glen to take a jacket with him in case it turned cool before they returned. They all went out to Manny's car. Glen sat in the back seat and fastened his seat belt. Manny put the popcorn on the back seat beside Glen before opening Mona's door for her and holding it while she got in and fastened her seat belt.

When they were on their way, Manny looked at Glen in the mirror and smiled. Glen looked so happy to be getting to go with them.

"Glen, do you know how to ride?" asked Manny.

Glen looked puzzled. "You mean horses?" asked Glen.

"Yes, I helped teach my nieces how to ride, and I was wondering if you would like to learn," said Manny.

"You helped teach your nieces how to ride?" asked Mona.

"Yes, Sam helped, too, but it was a team effort. It took a team to teach those girls. David and Lee have spoiled them. They are usually very sweet, but if they don't agree with you, they can make their opinion known," said Manny with a laugh.

"I would like to learn how to ride. Would it be okay, Mona?" asked Glen hopefully.

"I'll talk to Giles. I am sure it will be okay with him, but I have to ask first," said Mona.

"When your dad says it is okay, we will set up a time and you can come to the ranch for your lessons," said Manny.

"Thank you, Manny," said Glen.

When they arrived at the fire station and went inside, the Donaldson family was already there. The youngest boy was in Glen's class at school. They lost no time in teaming up. The fire truck had been placed outside so they would have more room to set up chairs for everyone to sit. They had extra folding chairs arranged in rows for seating. There was also a large beanbag chair for the boys to use.

Everyone was happy to smell the popcorn. "What's a movie without popcorn?" asked Leslie Donaldson.

The guys had moved the table back against the wall and everyone was putting their food on it. Manny took the box with the bags of popcorn in it and sat it in the center of the table. Glen went to pal around with the Donaldson boys, and Manny and Mona started making their way around the room and greeting everyone. They were introduced to the three firemen and their girlfriends. There was Spike who was with Trixie. Sloan's girlfriend was Amber. Lee was with Sadie. Mona made sure to introduce Manny to Babs and Wilson. Sylvia and Henry were running a little late. Henry had been a little late getting away from work. Sylvia had called Babs to let her know she was late but would be there. Stacy was there with Jason. The couples were paired off with each other. They all seemed to stay close together.

The guys had two ice chests filled with ice and sodas. Everyone was taking paper plates and filling them so they could eat during the movie. The boys were happy to fill their plates with a variety of foods. Each person also took a bag of popcorn and a soda.

"What movie are we going to be watching?" asked Chad Donaldson.

"We are going to watch *Speed*," said Captain Donaldson.

Some of the couples were sitting on the sofas. They were long, so two couples could sit on each sofa. Manny and Mona sat in chairs. They had scooted them close together so they could touch while watching the movie. As soon as Sylvia and Henry came in and filled a plate, Captain Donaldson turned most of the lights off and started the movie. Most of them had seen the movie before, but it was a favorite, and the group was having a great time.

After the movie, the lights were turned back on and

everyone was getting refills of food and drinks. They sat around, talking and relaxing. The boys were sprawled out on the beanbag chair talking and laughing. This had been a great idea for Glen, thought Mona.

She leaned closer to Manny, and he tightened his arm around her and smiled. "How many of the couples in this room were matched by the magic mirror?" asked Manny.

Mona looked around. "Babs saw Wilson. Stacy saw Jason. Sylvia saw Henry. With us, it makes four couples in this room who were matched by the magic mirror," said Mona.

"Wow," said Manny.

"Almost everyone in my group of friends has been matched by the magic mirror. Charise saw Zachery in the magic mirror. She was engaged to Sylvia's brother Arnold at the time. She broke her engagement and waited for Zachery to come home from assignment. He was on a mission with the Navy Seals."

"I know Katie saw Carlos and Star saw Sam," said Manny. He shook his head. The magic mirror has matched almost everyone in the town of Barons and Sharpville," said Manny.

Babs was close enough to hear his statement. "There ought to be a lot of happy marriages with the magic mirror only putting couples together who are true loves," said Babs.

"Yes," agreed Mona. "It also gives people the courage to take a chance on love. They may be holding back because they are afraid of failing or of it not lasting. When the magic mirror shows them their true love, they are free of worry and can enjoy the love."

"I am very thankful the magic mirror showed us we belonged together," said Manny, gazing at Mona.

"So am I," agreed Mona.

"I am thankful for each day I have with Wilson," said Babs.

"Did I hear my name?" asked Wilson, sliding his arm around Babs and kissing her.

"I was just telling Mona and Manny how happy I am the magic mirror brought you into my life," said Babs.

Wilson kissed her again. "So am I," he said. "So am I."

They hung around talking and eating until eight. When the Donaldson family started to get ready to go, Mona decided Glen needed to go home also. They wished everyone a good night, and Manny took the empty popcorn box and put it in the trunk of his car. He thought it might be needed again sometime.

In the car on the way home, Mona asked Glen if he had a good time. "It is the best time I have had ever," said Glen. "Can we do it again sometime?"

"They only have a movie night once a month, but I'm sure they won't mind you if you come the next time they have it," said Mona with a smile. Glen settled back and enjoyed the ride home.

When they reached the farm, Manny turned to look at Glen. "Don't forget, if it is okay with your folks, we are going to be having a riding lesson on Saturday," said Manny.

"Thanks, Manny, I won't forget. Thanks for taking me tonight. I had a great time," said Glen.

"You're welcome. You had better get inside and get ready for bed. I want to talk to Mona for a little while," said Manny.

"Okay, goodnight," said Glen as he undid his seat belt, left the car, and hurried to get inside the house.

Manny pulled Mona into his arms. Mona smiled. "So, we are going to talk, are we?"

"Right after I do this," said Manny as he kissed her deeply.

When they came up for air, Mona smiled at him. "I like the way you talk," she said, kissing him back.

They had been sitting there kissing and talking for about a half-hour when headlights of a car shined in as it passed by them and parked by the porch of the house. Giles got out. He looked their way and gave a little wave before going inside.

"I guess I have to let you go inside. I will be glad when we can be married, so I don't have to let you go," said Manny.

"Are you asking me to marry you, Mr. McCray?" asked Mona.

"Yes, I am," said Manny. "Are you going to say yes, Miss Santoes?"

"Yes, I am," said Mona kissing him again.

"When can we get married?" asked Manny.

"Whenever we can make the arrangements," said Mona. "Where are we going to live?"

"We need to live with my folks until I can get us a house built on the ranch. I need to be close so I can keep an eye on things at the ranch," said Manny.

"I like your mom. I don't think we will have any trouble getting along for a while. I need to keep an eye on Glen, too. I think he spends entirely too much time alone," said Mona.

"I knew you were worried about him. I thought the riding lessons were a way to get him out and let him have fun," said Manny.

"I appreciate you offering to teach him to ride. I think learning to ride will be very good for him," said Mona.

Manny kissed her again and sighed as he drew away. He got out of the car and came around and helped Mona out. They slowly walked to the front door. Manny drew to a stop at the door.

"Good night, my love," he said and kissed her again.

"Good night," whispered Mona as she turned and went inside.

Giles was in the kitchen eating when Mona came in.

47

Giles smiled at her. "Glen told me about going to the fire station with you and Manny. He was very happy about going."

"I think he had a good time visiting with the Donaldson boys," said Mona.

"He also said Manny has offered to teach him to ride," said Giles.

"Yes, I told Glen we would ask you if it was okay first," said Mona.

Giles shrugged. "It's fine. I think it will be good for him. With Jewel sick all of the time. He doesn't have anyone to talk to. Are you and Manny serious?" asked Giles.

"He asked me to marry him, and I said 'yes,'" said Mona.

"He seems to be a good person. I think you picked a winner," said Giles with a smile.

"The magic mirror picked him for me," said Mona.

"You saw him in the magic mirror at Danny's?" asked Giles.

Mona nodded. "Yes, I did."

"I am happy for you. I hope the best for you, and I think you have found him," said Giles.

"Thanks," said Mona with a smile.

"I'll say good night. I'll see you in the morning. I won't be going in tomorrow, so I can feed the kids," said Giles.

"Is something wrong at work?" asked Mona.

"No, they are doing inventory, so they gave us the next two days off while they count. They didn't want us in their way," said Giles.

"Good night, enjoy your break," said Mona.

Giles left to go upstairs.

CHAPTER 6

$\mathcal{M}$ona came down the next morning to find Giles in the kitchen. He had made breakfast and was putting it on the table. The girls and Glen were sitting at the table eating. They were ready for school. Mona told everyone good morning and took a plate and filled it with eggs, bacon, and toast. She had a glass of orange juice to drink.

"This is good, thanks, Giles," said Mona.

"You're welcome," said Giles with a smile.

They heard the bus blow its horn, and the kids hurried outside. Giles followed them out and watched them get on the bus. When he came back inside, Mona had finished her breakfast and was enjoying a cup of coffee.

Giles filled his cup with coffee and sat at the table with Mona. "I wanted to ask you about Jewel. Her headaches are getting worse. I've tried to get her to see a doctor, but she just says it is just a headache, so there is no need for a doctor. I don't know what else to do," said Giles.

"I know," said Mona. "I have tried to talk her into seeing a doctor, too. She either puts me off or ignores me."

Giles sighed. "I haven't tried to wake her up this morning. I am going to try again to get her to see a doctor while I am off and can go with her."

Mona got up to take her plate into the kitchen and clean it off and put it into the dishwasher. "Good luck. I hope you can convince her. I have to get to work. I have a client coming in early. She had an appointment and wanted to get her hair done before she went to it."

"Have a good day," said Giles.

"Thanks, enjoy your day off," said Mona.

Mona left and headed for the Cut and Curl.

Giles finished cleaning the dining room and kitchen. After he put the dishes in the dishwasher, he checked the kids' rooms and straightened the beds. He put the clothes in the dirty clothes basket. Giles sighed. He was stalling. He had to go and wake up Jewel. He went into their bedroom and went over and sat down on the bed beside Jewel. He gently shook her shoulder.

"Jewel, honey, wake up," said Giles. There was no response from Jewel. He shook her a little harder. "Jewel, wake up," said Giles. She still gave no response. Giles hurried downstairs and grabbed the phone and called 911.

"Hello, what is your emergency?" asked the operator.

"I can't get my wife to wake up. She is unresponsive," said Giles.

"I've got your address as the farm five miles from Barons," said the operator. "Is this correct?"

"Yes," agreed Giles.

"I am sending an ambulance to take her to the hospital in Sharpville. I am also sending the fire truck to see if they can help until the ambulance gets there. The fire truck is on its way," said the operator.

"I hear the siren," said Giles. He hung up the phone and hurried to open the door.

The fire truck stopped in front of the house. Wilson and Captain Donaldson hurried to the house carrying an emergency bag. Giles showed them the way to the bedroom and stood back and watched them check Jewel. They had a radio and were talking to the hospital on it.

"The patient is unresponsive," said Captain Donaldson. They listened to her heart and checked her eyes.

"Her pulse is slow, and her pupils have no activity and no response to light," said Wilson.

They heard another siren, and Giles hurried to let the ambulance medics in. They came into the room, and Wilson and Captain Donaldson moved back out of the way and watched the medics do the same thing they had just done.

"We are going to have to take her into the hospital," said one of the medics.

Giles nodded. "I'm going with you," said Giles.

"It would be better if you follow us in your car, so you will have it there if you need it," said the medic. "Your wife's condition is not going to change on the way to the hospital."

"Okay," agreed Giles. He watched them put Jewel into the back of the ambulance and then shut the door to the house and thanked Wilson and Captain Donaldson for coming out.

"If we can do anything to help, let us know," said Wilson.

"Could you go by the Cut and Curl and tell Mona that her mom is on her way to the hospital. I don't want to stop. I am going straight to the hospital," said Giles.

"Sure, we can tell her," said Wilson.

"Thanks," said Giles as he got in his car and headed for the hospital in Sharpville.

Wilson and Captain Donaldson headed back to Barons.

They stopped at the fire station, and Wilson got out and walked down to the Cut and Curl.

"Can I help you?" asked Hazel at the front desk.

"I need to speak with Mona Santoes," said Wilson.

"Her client has left. You can go on back," said Hazel.

Wilson went around the corner and spotted Mona cleaning her station. He headed for her.

Mona looked up and smiled when she saw Wilson. She stopped smiling when she saw his face. "Is something wrong?" she asked

"Your mom has been taken to the hospital in Sharpville. Your dad couldn't wake her up. She was unresponsive," said Wilson.

"Stepdad," Mona responded automatically. "Giles asked you to stop and tell me?"

"Yes, the fire department was asked to go out and check on her until the ambulance got there. Giles was going to the hospital and he asked if we would let you know," said Wilson.

"I have to get someone to cover my clients so I can go to the hospital," said Mona. "Thanks for letting me know."

"Sure. If we can help, let us know," said Wilson.

Mona nodded agreement, and Wilson left. Mona turned around and looked at her station. "Manny," she thought.

"What's wrong?" thought Manny.

"My mom has been taken to the hospital in Sharpville," thought Mona.

"I'll be right there. Are you at work?"

"Yes."

"Don't leave. I'm on my way," thought Manny.

"Okay."

Manny had been eating breakfast. He got up from the table and started to leave.

"Where are you going?" asked Cathy.

"They have taken Mona's mom to the hospital in Sharpville. I'm going to go and take her to the hospital," said Manny.

"How do you know?" asked Alvin.

"Mona just told me," said Manny, too distracted to explain further. "Mom if we are not back in time, would you meet the school bus and bring Mona's sisters and Glen over here until we get back?" asked Manny.

"Okay, tell Mona I will say a prayer for her mom," said Cathy.

"Thanks, Mom." Manny kissed her cheek and took off at a run to drive to Barons and pick up Mona.

Mona hurried to Pat's office to tell her she had to leave because her mom was in the hospital. "What's wrong with her?" asked Pat.

"I don't know. All I know is Giles had her taken to Sharpville by ambulance," said Mona. "I have two clients scheduled for today. Can you get someone to take care of them?" asked Mona.

"You go ahead," said Pat. "I'll take care of them."

"Thanks, Pat," said Mona.

"I hope Jewel is okay," said Pat.

"Thanks. Me too," said Mona.

Mona hurried to get her jacket and purse from her station and went outside. Manny pulled to a stop beside her when she came out. Mona hurried around and got into his car and they were on their way. Manny reached over and squeezed her hand. Mona felt much better for the contact. Having Manny there soothed her.

At the McCray ranch, after Manny left, Cathy looked at Alvin.

"Mona told him?" said Alvin.

Cathy grinned. "They mind talked," she said.

Alvin shook his head. "I have heard about it, but I haven't witnessed it before. Those two are made for each other."

"Yes, they are," agreed Cathy. "I guess I need to get some bedrooms ready in case Mona's brother and sisters have to stay over. I want to be prepared."

"I need to go and tell David to look after things while Manny is gone," said Alvin, getting up to leave. He came to Cathy's side and kissed her.

"Do you think we could do that mind talk?" asked Alvin.

Cathy smiled. "Anything is possible. We will have to try it out sometime," she said.

"Yeah," agreed Alvin with a grin.

He left to go outside, and Cathy went to check on the bedrooms. She was smiling to herself. She was definitely going to try out mind talking.

Mona and Manny arrived at the hospital in Sharpville. They were directed to the emergency waiting room when Mona asked about her mom. They found Giles sitting in the waiting room with his head down. He looked up when Mona and Manny entered the room.

"Is there any news?" asked Mona, hurrying over to him.

"No, they haven't told me anything, except she is in a coma and they are running tests to try and find out why," said Giles.

Mona turned into Manny's arms and he held her close. They sat in chairs close to Giles to wait. "Oh, Giles, this is Manny," said Mona.

"It's good to meet you, Sir. I hope your wife will be okay," said Manny.

"Thank you, it's nice to meet you, too," said Giles.

"I asked Mom to meet the school bus after school if we are not back. She is going to take the kids to our house until you can pick them up," said Manny.

Mona squeezed his hand. "Thanks, I hadn't even thought about the kids," said Mona.

"Thanks, Manny, I appreciate your help," said Giles.

"I just wanted to help. I was afraid you would think I was overstepping," said Manny.

"It's fine," said Giles. "You are part of the family. Mona told me you two are engaged," said Giles. "Congratulations, you have a great girl."

"I am very lucky to have her," said Manny, gazing into Mona's eyes with a smile.

The doctor came into the waiting room. They all rose to face him. "Mr. Santoes, we are transferring your wife to intensive care. She is still in a coma. We are going to have to run some more tests to find out why. In the meantime, we need her where she can be monitored closely. Only one person at a time may stay with her. We will let you know what is wrong as soon as we find out anything," said the doctor.

"Thank you, Doctor," said Giles.

"The nurse can show you the waiting room by intensive care so you will be closer to Mrs. Santoes," said the doctor. They went to ask a nurse to direct them to the intensive care waiting room.

Following her instructions, they headed toward the intensive care waiting room. As they passed the intensive care, someone came out the door and they saw Jewel, on a bed, being rolled into a room. She had wires hooked up to her, but she wasn't moving.

Mona felt tears well up in her eyes. She buried her head in Manny's chest and tried to control her tears. Giles looked away and battled his own tears. Manny held Mona close and tried to comfort her.

Giles went over and knocked on the door of intensive care and asked if he could go to Jewel's room. The nurse allowed him in and told Mona and Manny they could wait in the waiting room next door. They could be allowed in to see Jewel later.

Manny guided Mona into the waiting room, and they choose a sofa to sit on so they could be close together. "I knew something was wrong," said Mona. "She kept getting bad headaches. I tried to get her to see a doctor, but she wouldn't go. She kept saying it was just a headache, it would get better."

"There was nothing you could do if she didn't want to see a doctor," said Manny. "She is a grown woman. She has to decide for herself as long as she is able. In cases like this, the husband can decide for her. This coma may be the best thing to happen to her. She can get the help she needs and get better."

"I hope so," said Mona. "Thanks for thinking about my sisters and Glen. I hadn't even thought about them."

Manny put an arm around her and hugged her close. "I knew you were only thinking about your mom. I am here for you; anything you need, just ask." Mona smiled and snuggled close to his side.

Giles was sitting in Jewel's room and watching the nurses and the doctor hook Jewel up to various machines. The doctor left after ordering more tests. The nurses started leaving one at a time after they finished the tests they were doing. The last one smiled at Giles reassuringly. Giles moved his chair over closer to the side of the bed and reached for Jewel's hand.

"You have to get better, Jewel," said Giles. "I need you. The girls and Glen need you. Mona needs you, too. You have to help her plan her wedding to Manny. They are so happy together. They remind me of us when I finally managed to get you to forget about Mario and marry me. We were so happy. You and I should have been together all along, but I can't regret your marriage to him because he gave you Mona. She is a great person. We were a family before the girls and Glen came along. She has been a great big sister. She looks after Glen like he was her own, and he adores her. When you get out of here, we are going to start taking some time off to enjoy our time with the kids. We could go camping, picnicking, swimming, and maybe even to movies sometimes, all of the things we used to do with Mona when we were first married, before the girls and Glen came along."

Giles choked up and paused for a minute to clear his throat. He squeezed Jewel's hand again and gazed at her and prayed not to lose the love of his life. He and the kids needed her. She was the glue that kept the family together. He didn't want to even think of a life without her. Giles held onto Jewel's hand and kept talking to her softly. Maybe somehow, she could hear him and know she was not alone. He never wanted her to feel alone. She had told him once: the greatest fear of her childhood was of being alone. As long as he was able, she was not going to feel alone.

The time passed slowly for Mona and Manny as they sat waiting for news. They had been sitting there waiting for over an hour when Giles came into the room. Mona and Manny hurried over to him. "Is Mom alright?" asked Mona.

"There has been no change," said Giles. "They came in to take her somewhere for a scan and some more tests. They told me to wait here, so I thought I would come out and let you know what is going on."

"I guess all we can do is wait until they tell us what is going on," said Mona.

"Could we go out in the hall to talk? I want to be where I can see when they come back up," said Giles.

They went out in the hall. They stayed close to the waiting room door so they would not be in anyone's way. Giles kept his eyes glued to the door they would be bringing Jewel through.

CHAPTER 7

They finally brought Jewel back to intensive care. Giles followed them into her room. He asked the orderly if there was any news, but the orderly told him he just transported the patient. The doctor would have to give him the results. Giles sat down at Jewel's bedside and held her hand as he resumed talking to her.

The doctor finally came by. He told Giles the tests were inconclusive. There would have to be further tests. Giles went out and told Mona and Manny what the doctor had said. He let Mona go in and sit with her mom for a while, and he stayed in the waiting room with Manny.

"Would you like some coffee or something to eat?" asked Manny.

"No," said Giles. "My stomach is tied up in knots. I couldn't eat anything. When Mona comes out, see if she will go down to the cafeteria for something. It is well past lunchtime," said Giles.

"I'll try," said Manny.

Mona came back in the waiting room, and Giles went back into Jewel's room.

After Giles was gone, Mona hugged Manny. "She is so still. I don't know what to say to her. It breaks my heart to see her like this," whispered Mona.

"I know," said Manny holding her and trying to comfort her.

"Would you like to go down to the cafeteria? We can get some coffee, and I can check with Mom and see if she picked up your sisters and Glen," said Manny.

"Okay," agreed Mona.

They left the waiting room and made their way to the cafeteria. They ordered a coffee, and Manny picked up a couple of muffins. When they were at their table, Manny called his mom.

"I was just about to call you," said Cathy. "I picked up Glen and Poppie, but Glen and Poppie told me Beth had gone home with her friend Erin."

"Just a minute, Mom," said Manny.

Manny turned to Mona. "Mom said she picked up Glen and Poppie, but Beth went home with her friend Erin," said Manny.

Mona frowned. She held out her hand for the phone. "Hello, Mrs. McCray," said Mona softly. "Manny said Beth went to her friend Erin's house."

"Yes," said Cathy. "Poppie didn't want to say anything, but Glen said Beth told them she had permission from their mom to spend the night with Erin."

"Thanks for picking up Poppie and Glen. I'll take care of Beth," said Mona.

"Okay, Dear. Is there any word on your mom?" asked Cathy.

"Not yet, they are still running tests. She is still in a coma," said Mona.

"I'll be praying for you all. If you need anything, call me," said Cathy.

"I will, thank you," said Mona.

Mona turned off the phone and handed it to Manny. She took out her phone and found Sharon, Erin's mom. She punched in the send button.

"Hello, Mona," said Sharon. "Would you like to speak to Beth?"

"Yes, but first, I need to ask you if it is okay for Beth to stay with you for a few days. Mom is in the hospital in a coma. I had made arrangements for the kids to stay with the McCrays, but since Beth is already there, I was hoping she could stay until I can come and get her," said Mona.

"Sure, however long you need. She is welcome. Let me know if there is anything I can do to help," said Sharon.

"Thanks, Sharon. Now, may I speak to Beth?"

"Mona," said Beth. "I did have permission to stay at Erin's tonight. I asked Mom if it was alright."

"Let me guess, she didn't say anything, so you decided to go ahead and do what you wanted to do," said Mona quietly so the people in the cafeteria did not hear her.

"What's the big deal? I just wanted to visit with Erin," said Beth

"The big deal is you did not tell either your dad or myself you were going. Mom did not give you permission to go. She couldn't because she is in the hospital in a coma. You are a liar, and you left your sister and your brother to come home alone. You did not know if anyone was there for them or not. You are going to stay at Erin's until I can come and get you. When I do come after you, you and I are going to have a talk."

"Can I talk to Dad?" asked Beth.

"Do you honestly think I am going to pull him away from

Mom's bedside just so you can moan to him and get your way? It's not going to happen. You be good for Erin's mom and do as she says. I'll be in touch." Mona hung up her phone and sighed.

She looked at Manny. He was watching her with a grin. "It sounds like Beth is a Daddy's girl," said Manny.

"Yeah, she has him wrapped around her finger, but this is one time she is not going to use Giles to get out of trouble. Her actions could have had serious consequences. She needs to know she can't always do just what she wants to."

Manny pulled her close. "Just take it easy and don't do anything while you are so stressed out," said Manny.

"Okay," said Mona with a small smile. "Can we go back to intensive care?"

"Sure," agreed Manny. He wrapped two muffins in napkins to take with them.

Giles came out to the waiting room shortly after they returned from the cafeteria. "The doctor said he would be out to talk to me after he finishes checking out your mom," said Giles. "He said they do not like talking in front of the patients in comas because they don't know how much they hear and understand."

Mona just nodded. "Poppie and Glen are with Mrs. McCray. Beth went home with Erin. I talked to Sharon and she said she would keep Beth until we come and get her," said Mona. Giles looked surprised at the information about Beth, but he didn't say anything. He was preoccupied with what the doctor would say.

The wait seemed forever, but finally, the doctor came into the waiting room looking for them. He came over and sat in a chair next to Giles.

"Mr. Santoes, your wife has a tumor on her brain stem. It has been causing her headaches. It has to be removed. We have put out a call for a surgeon who specializes in this type of surgery. We are waiting to hear back from him. There are still a lot of tests we have to do before surgery can be attempted. If you have friends with Jewel's blood type, please ask them to donate blood. She is type B. We need to stock up. The hospital is in short supply. Other types will be accepted as well. If the person donating tells the person taking the blood it is for Jewel, it will help keep the cost of blood transfusions down. This surgery is going to be very expensive. You can go by the business office and take all of your insurance information, and they can give you an estimate on the cost above what the insurance will pay. They can also help you apply for aid in paying the costs."

"Is my wife going to be alright after she has this surgery?" asked Giles.

"She has a good chance of a full recovery. If she doesn't have the surgery, she will never wake up from the coma," said the doctor.

"How soon will she be able to have this surgery?" asked Mona.

"It will depend on the surgeon. I would say it will probably be one day next week. He may be able to get here by next Monday or Tuesday," said the doctor.

"Won't it be dangerous for my mom to have to wait so long? Today is Thursday," said Mona.

"We are keeping her regulated and in the coma. As long as she doesn't wake up, she won't get any worse," said the doctor. He stood up. "I'll let you know as soon as I hear from the surgeon."

"Thank you, Doctor," said Giles.

The doctor left, and they all sat down, trying to digest what they had been told.

"Charise's wedding is Saturday. I need to let her know I can't be there," said Mona.

Giles shook his head. "Jewel would want you to be there. Take lots of pictures for her to look at when she is better. She will love knowing her little girl got to meet the Governor and a Senator. She would be so disappointed if she made you miss it," said Giles.

Mona looked undecided, but then reluctantly nodded. She squeezed Manny's hand. "Do you think I should go?" she asked.

"Well, you did promise to do their hair and makeup. We don't have to stay long. We can leave as soon as they make their toasts. I'm sure Charise and Zachery will understand," said Manny.

"Okay," said Mona. "Do you need us to do anything, Giles?"

"Will you go and get the folder Jewel keeps all of our insurance information in and bring it to me in the morning? Check on the kids and let them know what is going on. I wouldn't want them to find out at school tomorrow," said Giles.

"Okay," agreed Mona. "Do you want me to bring you a change of clothes?"

"Yes, I'll doze in the chair in Jewel's room. I'll see you in the morning" said Giles.

Manny and Mona gave Giles a hug before leaving. Manny gave Giles the muffins he had wrapped in napkins. Giles didn't want to take them at first but shrugged and accepted them. Giles watched them go before going back into Jewel's room.

Manny held Mona close to his side as they went down to his car. When they were in the car on the way to Barons, Mona called Pat at the Cut and Curl and told her what was going on. She also asked her to spread the word about the blood donations. Pat said she would tell everyone first thing in the morning. Most of the ladies had left for the day. Mona thanked her and hung up. She lay back in her seat and sighed. Manny looked at her with concern.

"It is going to be alright," he said.

Mona looked at him and smiled. "I love you," she said. "I am so happy I don't have to go through this without you," she said.

"I love you, too. I will always be here when you need me," said Manny.

They went to the ranch first to check on Poppie and Glen. When they came in the door, both Poppie and Glen ran over and hugged Mona. Then Glen hugged Manny. "Mrs. McCray told us Mom was sick," said Poppie.

"Yes, she is in the hospital in Sharpville. Your dad is with her," said Mona.

"What's wrong with her?" asked Poppie.

Mona led the kids over to the sofa and sat down with them on either side of her. She put an arm around each one and tried to be as reassuring as she could.

"Mom is in a coma. When your dad couldn't wake her up, he called an ambulance and had her taken to the hospital. They ran a bunch of tests on her and found she had a tumor. It's what has been causing her headaches. They have sent for a surgeon to take the tumor out. They are not going to try and wake her up until the surgeon removes the tumor. The doctors are waiting to see when the surgeon will get here," said Mona.

"Is Mom going to get better?" asked Glen.

Mona gave him an extra hug. "Mom is going to be fine. When she wakes up, she won't have headaches anymore. When you say your prayers tonight, ask for her to be looked after and to get well soon," said Mona.

"Okay," agreed Glen.

"I'll say a prayer for her, too," said Poppie.

Mona gave both of them a hug. "I have to go over to the house and pick up some insurance papers and some clothes for your dad. Is there anything I need to get for either of you?" Mona looked at Cathy. "I should have asked if it was alright for them to stay here with you for a few more days." She said.

Cathy waved her hand. "It's fine. I already have their rooms arranged."

"Thank you," said Mona.

"Could you bring my tablet?" asked Poppie.

"Okay," agreed Mona.

"You are welcome to stay, also," said Cathy.

"I don't know," said Mona, looking at Manny.

Manny grinned at Mona. "I don't think she means to put you in my room," he said with a grin.

"Absolutely not," said Cathy. "You are not married yet."

"I know, Mom," said Manny. "I was just teasing."

"You bring Mona back over with you. Don't let her stay over there by herself," said Cathy.

"I'll try," said Manny.

"Have you two had anything to eat?" asked Cathy.

"No, we weren't hungry," said Manny.

"You two wash up. I'll get some food ready," said Cathy.

Mona smiled at Manny as they got up to follow Cathy's orders. Poppie and Glen followed them into the dining room. Cathy fixed them a plate each and sat them on the table. Mona looked at the plate piled high with food and then looked at Manny.

Manny shook his head. "Just eat what you can," he said with a grin. He picked up his fork and started eating, and Mona followed his guide.

"This is good," said Mona as she started eating. They sat

talking and eating until Mona looked down in surprise to see her plate empty.

She flushed slightly. "I guess I was hungrier than I thought," said Mona.

"You haven't eaten all day, and you were, very, stressed. You needed to refuel," said Cathy.

They stood, and Mona started to gather their plates. "Just leave those," said Cathy. "You two go and get what you need to pick up. I'll have your room ready when you get back," said Cathy.

CHAPTER 8

On the way to Mona's house, Mona decided to go by and check on Beth. When Sharon opened her door, she smiled and said, "Hi," to Manny and gave Mona a hug, as she asked about Jewel.

"Hi," said Manny.

"Mom is still in a coma. She has a brain tumor. They are going to keep her in a coma until she can be operated on. The doctor has sent for a surgeon. She will probably be operated on next week," said Mona.

Beth came into the room with Erin. As soon as she saw Mona, she burst into tears and ran over and hugged her. Mona held her close and comforted her while she cried. "I'm sorry. I didn't know Mom was so sick. I know I shouldn't have come over to Erin's without talking to you or Dad first. I was being very selfish and only thinking about myself. I'm sorry," said Beth.

Mona pulled away slightly and looked down at Beth. "Mom has a brain tumor. She is going to have an operation." Mona looked at Beth sternly. "Coming to Erin's is not the problem. You have to let your dad or I know when you are going somewhere. We cannot have you going off on your own without letting us know. It is too dangerous. You know your dad would have given you permission if you had asked him. You chose not to ask. I have asked Erin's mom if you can stay here a few days. Poppie and Glen are staying with Mrs. McCray. I will let you know how Mom is as soon as I can," explained Mona.

Beth nodded her head. "I'll be good and help Erin clean her room," promised Beth.

Sharon laughed. "If you can get Erin to straighten her room, I just might invite you over more often. It is the one chore she hates." She gave Erin a hug and a smile. "Beth, you are welcome to stay as long as you need to, but next time I think I'll need to have Mona or one of your parents call me first," said Sharon.

"Yes, Ma'am," said Beth looking down sheepishly.

"Thanks, Sharon," said Mona. She gave Beth another hug and turned to Manny.

"Manny and I have to go and pick up some things for Giles. If you get a chance, would you spread the word around that Mom needs blood donations? She is type B."

"Sure," said Sharon. "I'll get the word out."

"Can I donate blood?" asked Beth.

"No," said Mona smiling. "You are not old enough," Mona smiled at her. "I am sure Mom will be happy to hear you wanted to give blood. I'll be sure to tell her when she is better."

Beth gave her another hug before Mona and Manny left to go to the farmhouse, after telling Sharon, Erin, and Beth goodbye.

They went in and Mona collected the insurance papers while Manny put together a small bag of clothes and a few necessary items for Giles. Mona gathered some clothes for

Poppie, Glen, and herself. She included Poppie's tablet and a toy for Glen. They went down to the kitchen and checked to be sure everything was turned off and locked up.

When they were ready to go, Mona turned into Manny's arms and hugged him tight. "I love you. Thank you for letting me work through things with Beth," she said.

Manny smiled down into her eyes. "I knew you were just worried about her, and I knew the two of you would work it out. You have been an influence on her from the day she was born. She might stray, but she will always come back to the values you have shown her all of her life. She is a good kid in a stressful situation. I am very proud of the way you handled the situation," said Manny, kissing her gently.

Mona hugged him tightly and raised her face for another kiss. Manny kissed her but pulled back when they heard a car stopping in front of the house.

They opened the door and found Charise and Zachery getting out of their car. Charise hurried over and gave Mona a hug. Zachery nodded at Manny and smiled at Mona.

"I heard about your mom and I wanted to see if there was anything I could do to help," said Charise.

Mona shook her head. "There is nothing to do but wait. They are waiting on a surgeon. The operation will be next week if we can get everything worked out."

"I wanted to see if you wanted to skip my wedding since you have so much going on," said Charise. "I would completely understand if you do."

"No," said Mona shaking her head. "I will do the hair and makeup for everyone. It will help me to keep busy. Manny and I may have to leave a little early if it's okay."

"It's fine. I want to make sure we are not pressuring you," said Charise.

"There is one thing," said Mona. "Giles said I should get

some pictures to show Mom when she's better. Do you think you could have some extra pictures made for me?"

"Of course, I'll have the photographer print an extra set of pictures and send them to you," agreed Charise.

"I can see you two were on your way out; I'll let you go. I hope your mom will be alright." She started to leave and turned back. "Don't worry about the rehearsal tomorrow. Just come to my house on Saturday morning. I'm sure you know what to do, and we can all show you if you don't," said Charise.

Mona smiled at Charise and Zachery. "Thank you both for coming by. If you know anyone with type B blood, ask them to go by the hospital and donate for Jewel Santoes."

"I'll spread the word," agreed Charise.

"I'll tell the guys at the gym," said Zachery.

"Thanks," said Mona. She and Manny stood watching as Charise and Zachery left.

Mona looked up at Manny and smiled. "Everyone is being so nice. I'm almost afraid I'll wake up and find this is all a dream."

Manny hugged her. "You are easy to be nice to. I think a lot of people are nice to you just to see your beautiful smile."

"I think you are prejudice," said Mona.

"Yes, I am," agreed Manny. "I love you and I am glad you are mine."

They left to return to the McCray home. Mona gave Poppie and Glen their things and left her clothes in the room Cathy had arranged for her. When she returned to the living room, she found Manny and Alvin talking about the day. Alvin was catching Manny up on ranch business and Manny was updating Alvin on Jewel's condition.

Alvin rose when Mona came in. He took her hands and squeezed them lightly. "I'm sorry about your mom, Mona. If there is anything we can do to help, just let us know," he smiled. "You are part of our family now, and we want to help."

"Thank you," said Mona. "Letting Glen and Poppie stay here is a big help."

Alvin shrugged. "They are no problem. It will be nice to have youngsters around again. All of our boys have grown, and we don't get to spend near about enough time with David's girls. It seems like they are always busy." Alvin glanced at Manny with a grin. "I don't remember you boys having so many after school activities."

"We spent most of our after-school time working on the ranch," said Manny with a smile.

Alvin nodded. "You all loved working with the horses," he agreed.

Cathy came into the room. "Poppie is glued to her tablet. I think she missed it," she said.

Mona laughed as she went close to Manny, and he put an arm around her and drew her close to his side. "She does love it. She would take it to school with her, but Mom put her foot down. Poppie was told she is never allowed to take her tablet to school. School is for schoolwork, but as long as she does her homework, she can have her tablet at home."

Cathy nodded. "I'll remember if she tries to take it to school," she said.

Mona smiled. "We are putting a lot on you," she said. "I really appreciate you helping."

Cathy shrugged and came over and sat by Alvin. He smiled and put his arm around her. "It's been nice having them here. I am glad for a chance to get to know your family. We will all be praying for your mom's recovery."

"Thank you," said Mona. "If you don't mind, I need to try and get a little sleep. I want to get to the hospital early tomorrow. I thought I could leave after the bus runs."

"I called the school and asked them to pick up Glen and Poppie here for a few days," said Cathy.

"Thanks," said Mona. "I didn't think about the bus."

Cathy nodded. "You go on up and try to rest. We will see you in the morning."

"Good night," said Mona.

"I'll walk you up," said Manny, taking her hand and leading the way.

They stopped in front of Mona's door, and Manny drew her close and kissed her. When they came up for air, Mona leaned her forehead into his chest. Manny gave her one last squeeze and pulled back.

"You go on in and try to sleep," he said. "I'll take you to the hospital in the morning. Try not to worry."

"I'll try," said Mona. She gave him a quick kiss and went into her room. Mona turned and smiled at Manny as she closed her door.

Manny sighed and went on down the hall to his room. After a quick shower, they both put on nightclothes and climbed into bed

Mona lay back and closed her eyes. They popped back open. She was too tired to sleep. Manny was having a similar problem. "Manny are you there?" thought Mona.

"I'm here," thought Manny.

"I am too tired to sleep," thought Mona.

"Maybe if we talk a bit, you can unwind and get sleepy," thought Manny.

"Maybe," sighed Mona. "What do you want to talk about?"

"How about we talk about our wedding," suggested Manny.

"Okay," agreed Mona.

"I won't push for a date until your mom is better, but as

soon as she is, I want to start our life together. I want to be able to sleep with you in my arms, close by my side," thought Manny.

"I want that, too," agreed Mona. "I hate having to leave your side and go into my room alone."

"It won't be all sleeping," thought Manny with a grin. "I am going to make love to you until we both have trouble breathing."

"If this is supposed to be relaxing me, I think you are using the wrong cure. I don't feel at all relaxed," thought Mona.

Manny grinned. "You have to admit it is a great stress reliever."

"I don't feel stressed out. I feel hot and itchy," thought Mona.

Manny groaned. "I wish I could help you scratch the itch, but my mom would have a fit if I sneaked into your room."

Mona giggled.

"You can laugh. My mom is ferocious when we break her rules," thought Manny.

"I would never do anything to upset your mom. She is a sweetheart," thought Mona.

"Yes, she is," agreed Manny.

"I think I can sleep now," thought Mona. "I love you."

"I love you, too. If you need me just call," thought Manny

Cathy and Alvin were sitting quietly, talking. He had his arm around her, and she was leaning her head on his chest.

"I love you," thought Cathy.

"I love you, too," thought Alvin.

Cathy sat up, grinning at Alvin. "We mind talked," she said.

Alvin looked at her, startled. Then he started grinning. "Yes, we did," he agreed.

He pulled her close for a kiss. When they came up for air, Alvin looked into her eyes lovingly. "I always knew we were meant for each other. Who needs a magic mirror to tell them when they find true love? I always knew you were my true love," said Alvin.

"Me. too, I knew the first time I saw you we were meant to be together. You have always been the only person for me." agreed Cathy.

Alvin hugged Cathy one more time before they rose to go to their room. Cathy waited by the stairs while Alvin checked the doors and turned the lights off. When he joined her at the stairs, they climbed the stairs together. Alvin had his arm around Cathy, and she was held close to his side.

They entered their room and shut the rest of the world out.

CHAPTER 9

Cathy was already in the kitchen the next morning, when Mona entered the room. Glen and Poppie were digging into large plates of pancakes. Manny was seated at the table enjoying his own stack of pancakes.

Cathy glanced at Mona when she entered the room. "Good morning. Have a seat," she said. She set a plate of pancakes in front of Mona.

Mona looked at the stack of pancakes and groaned. "I will never be able to eat all of these," said Mona. She took a deep breath. "They smell so good." Mona picked up her fork and dug in.

Cathy smiled as she poured Mona a cup of coffee and set it down by her plate. Mona smiled and thanked her. Poppie and Glen finished eating and went to wash their hands and collect their school bags. Mona smiled at Cathy. "I did not mean to make you cook for us," she said.

"I like cooking. I miss having children around to cook for," said Cathy.

The school bus horn blew, and Mona hurried out to tell Poppie and Glen goodbye. She followed them out to the bus.

She explained to the driver about their mom and thanked her for her condolences. Mona waved Glen and Poppie off as the bus pulled away.

Jimmy and Steve were also on the bus and watched as Glen and Poppie took their seats. They were curious about what was going on but decided to avoid making Manny mad at them. They could see Manny was fond of Glen, and they didn't want to spend any additional time cleaning the barn.

Mona went back inside to find Manny waiting for her. He had helped Cathy clean the kitchen and was ready to take Mona to the hospital. They told Cathy goodbye and went out to Manny's car.

When they reached the hospital, Mona went by the office to show them the insurance papers. The lady in the office took the insurance papers to look over and make copies and gave Mona some papers to fill out. She and Manny went over to the chairs and sat down while Mona filled everything out, then she took the forms back to the desk. The lady handed her the insurance papers. She made copies of the papers Mona filled out and gave her the copies.

"Mr. Santoes will have to come by the office and sign the papers, also," said the lady.

"Okay, I'll tell him," agreed Mona.

"Your insurance will pay about half of the cost of the operation. It is a very expensive operation. One of the papers you filled out is a request for state aid. We will submit it for you. Even with aid, there will be a substantial bill," said the lady.

"We will have to set up a payment plan," said Mona. "I'll tell my stepdad, and he can talk to you about it when he comes to sign the papers. It won't postpone the operation, will it?"

"No, as long as you have insurance, the operation will go ahead. We will figure out the rest later," she assured Mona.

"Good," said Mona. "Thank you for your help."

Mona and Manny left the office and headed upstairs. Manny put an arm around her and gave her a reassuring squeeze. "Don't worry. It will all work out," said Manny.

Mona gave him a weak smile. "I know, it is just one more thing to worry about when we should be able to concentrate on Mom getting the help she needs."

"Let's just hope they have been able to get the doctor scheduled," said Manny.

They approached intensive care and looked for Giles. The nurse went to get him, and he came out to talk to them. "How is Mom?" asked Mona after giving Giles a hug.

"She's the same. The doctor came by. He said the surgeon is scheduled for next Tuesday," said Giles. "Did you get the insurance papers?"

"Yes," said Mona. "I took them by the office and filled out some forms. One is a request for aid in paying the bill. The lady in the office said you would have to come by and sign the papers. The insurance will only cover about half of the bill. Even with financial aid, there will still be a large bill."

Giles rubbed his hand over his face. "We will figure it out later. Right now, we just have to get Jewel better."

"Would you like me to stay with Mom while you go by the office and get you something to eat? You could go home and stretch out and rest a little," said Mona.

"They have been bringing me food from the cafeteria," said Giles.

"You still need to go and take a break. If there is any change, I will call you at once," said Mona.

"Okay," said Giles. "I'll go and talk to them in the office and get a meal. Did you bring my clothes?"

"Yes, Manny has your bag. If you need anything else, just

let me know. The kids are doing okay. Beth wanted to donate blood. I told her she wasn't old enough," said Mona.

Giles smiled. "Jewel will love to hear about Beth wanting to help," said Giles. "I'll see you in a while. Call me if you need me."

"I will," assured Mona as she watched Giles leave.

Mona turned to Manny. "Are you going to wait, or do you have errands to run?" she asked.

Manny handed her Giles' bag. "I am going to go over to Coffee and Sweets and talk to Katie. When I get back, I'll wait in the waiting room."

"Okay," Mona raised her face for a kiss and, after receiving her kiss, turned and gave Manny a small wave as she entered the door to go to Jewel's room. She took Giles' bag and left it on a chair. She then went over and sat next to the bed. Mona took Jewel's hand and gave it a squeeze.

"I love you, Mom. We are all praying for you to get well. Beth is staying with Erin, and Poppie and Glen are with Mrs. McCray. They are all being spoiled. They would all be having the time of their lives if they were not worried about you. Beth even wanted to donate blood for you. I had to tell her she wasn't old enough. I won't be here tomorrow. I will be going to Charise's wedding. I started to cancel, but Giles convinced me to go and get lots of pictures to show you later. He said you would want to see your daughter meeting the Governor and Senator Willis. I have to admit it is something I never thought would happen to me. Manny is going with me. When you are better, Manny and I are going to be married. I love him, Mom. He is the one true love meant just for me. I saw him in the magic mirror at Danny's. He loves me just as much as I love him. You are going to love him, too. He is the sweetest person. He makes me feel safe and excited at the same time. I am looking forward to being his wife.

"We will be living at the McCray ranch until we can build a house. I will still be close enough to help you with the kids while you are getting better. Manny has promised Glen he will teach him to ride. Glen has always loved horses. He is excited about this chance to learn more about them and getting to ride. I guess I should stop talking so much and let you rest. I'll be right here with you until Giles gets back. You are not alone. We will make sure of that."

Mona got up and wandered over to the window and looked out. From the window, she could see the town in the distance. She could see the cars going up and down the streets. They were too far away to see them clearly, but it was something to think of so much going on just a short distance away. It almost seemed like the hospital was its own community. It was apart from the town, but it was also a part of the town. It was strange to be here and listen to the sounds of the doctors and nurses hurrying around. They were busy doing what they could to help the patients. They were so used to this hospital community they didn't even notice it anymore. It was commonplace to them.

Mona sighed. She turned and went back over to check on her mom. She picked up a magazine to look at. If she stayed here much, she would bring a book to read. She sat down to look at the magazine and wait for Giles to come back.

Manny went into town and stopped at Coffee and Sweets. Katie was just bringing out a tray of apple tarts when she looked up and spotted him. She started smiling and hurried over to give him a hug.

"What are you doing in town?" asked Katie.

"I am here with Mona. She is at the hospital with her mom," said Manny.

"I heard about Mona's mom having to have an operation," said Katie.

"Yes, the operation is scheduled for next Tuesday," said Manny. "The reason I came by was to see if you could spread the word about Jewel Santoes needing type B blood. Ask if anyone with type B would go by the hospital and donate. She is going to need quite a bit for surgery."

"I'm already ahead of you," said Katie. "Carlos heard about it at Fitness Central. I have already put up a sign, and we have been encouraging our customers to donate," said Katie.

"Thanks," said Manny grinning at her.

"You are welcome. How serious are you and Mona?" she asked.

"I asked her to marry me. She said 'yes.' As soon as her mom is better, we are going to be married," said Manny.

"I am so happy for you," said Katie, giving him a hug.

"Thank you," said Manny. He turned and looked at the sound of the door opening. Manny grinned when he saw Carlos come in. Those two could not stay away from each other for long. It was a good thing they worked so close together. Manny was looking forward to being that close to Mona. He had only been away from her for a little while, and he missed being close to her.

"Hello," said Carlos after he kissed Katie. "How is Mona's mom?"

"She is the same. They are going to keep her in a coma until Tuesday, when she will have the tumor removed," said Manny. "They are dealing with the cost now. Their insurance is only going to pay for half of the cost. It leaves them with having to come up with the other half."

"Are they applying for state aid?" asked Katie.

"Yes, they have to wait and see how much it will help," said Manny.

Carlos shook his head. "Give Mona our best wishes and tell her we will be praying for her mom."

"I will tell her," promised Manny.

"Manny and Mona are engaged," said Katie.

Carlos grinned and shook Manny's hand. "Congratulations," he said.

"Thank you," said Manny, smiling. "I'll see you both later. I have to get back to the hospital. Mona stayed with her mom to give Giles a break."

Katie gave him another hug, and Carlos patted him on his back and shook his hand. Manny gave a small wave to Star and Bambi as he went out the door. They both waved back at him.

"We need to spread the word about Jewel needing financial help." said Katie.

Carlos nodded. "We need to be discrete. We don't want to step on any toes. We don't want to get another feud started."

"No, we don't," agreed Katie with a shiver.

Carlos drew her into his arms. "Don't worry, we will find a way to help."

Manny went back to the waiting room in intensive care. He settled back in a chair and looked around. He almost had the room to himself. There was only one other person there.

Manny leaned back in his chair and thought about Mona. "Hello, Love," he thought. "I'm back in the waiting room."

"Hi, I'm glad you are back. I like having you close," thought Mona.

"I talked to Katie. She is already spreading the word about your mom needing type B blood. Carlos told her. Zachery had told everyone at the gym," thought Manny.

"I'll have to check downstairs and see if they are getting enough blood donated," thought Mona. "It's nice to have so many friends and family helping out."

"I think I'll go down and donate," thought Manny. "I'll ask how they are doing while I am there."

"Okay, thanks," thought Mona. "I'll go down when Giles gets back."

"Do you want me to wait and go with you?" thought Manny.

"No, I don't know how long Giles is going to be. It will give you something to do besides just sitting there waiting. I love you. Thanks for helping my mom," thought Mona.

"I love you, too. I'll be back soon," thought Manny.

Manny rose and started for the elevator for the first floor. He found the blood bank and went inside. The nurse inside smiled at him. "Can I help you?" she asked.

"I wanted to see about donating blood for Jewel Santoes," said Manny.

"Okay, do you know your blood type?" she asked.

"I think I am type O. I was told I could be a universal donor," said Manny.

"Yes, if we don't get enough type B, we can use type O."

"Have you had many type B donations?" asked Manny.

"We have had one so far. Jewel's friends from the hair salon came in. One of them was type B. Two were type O. The rest were type A," said the nurse.

While they had been talking, the nurse had been setting up and drawing Manny's blood. When she finished, she put a bandage on the spot on his arm and handed him a glass of orange juice.

"Just sit back and relax for a few minutes," the nurse told him. She took the vial of blood in the other room to refrigerate it. Manny sat back and drank his juice.

While he was sitting there, Alvin and Cathy entered the room. Manny looked at them in surprise.

"What are you guys doing here?" asked Manny.

Alvin grinned at him. "The same thing you are doing. We wanted to help."

"Yes, we decided to come over while the kids are in school," agreed Cathy.

Manny got up and went over and hugged both of his parents. "You guys are the best," said Manny. "Thanks."

"Have they set the date for the surgery?" asked Cathy.

"Yes, it's Tuesday," said Manny.

"We went by the business office before we came here," said Alvin.

"We know how expensive an operation can be," said Cathy. "So, we started a fund to help pay for it. We opened it with a thousand dollars. We don't want to tell Mona. She may not want to take our money. We are going to encourage our friends and neighbors to contribute to the fund."

Manny looked at his parents misty-eyed. "You guys are the best," he repeated and gave them another hug.

"I think you will find a lot of people will want to help," said Cathy. "All they need is for someone to tell them how."

The nurse came back in and prepared to take their blood. Manny waited with them. When they were finished, they all went up to the waiting room. Manny had informed Mona, on the way up in the elevator, of his parent's arrival and blood donations. She was waiting in front of the door to the waiting room when they got off the elevator.

Mona came forward, as soon as she saw Alvin and Cathy, and gave each of them a hug. "Thank you so much for donating blood," said Mona.

"The nurse in the blood bank said they have only had one type B donation so far, but there are several type O donations. If they don't get enough type B, they can use type O," said Manny. "The type B was from one of the ladies at Cut and Curl."

"When this is all over, I'll have to do something nice for the ladies," said Mona.

"We just wanted to drop by and see how everything was going," said Cathy. "We had better head for home. We don't want the kids to come home to an empty house."

"We'll see you later," said Manny. There was another round of hugs as his parents left.

CHAPTER 10

The next morning Manny drove Mona to Charise's house and dropped her off. The girls were all going to meet there and get their hair and makeup done before going to the country club at one. The wedding was to be at two. Charise had made arrangements for a limo to take them to the country club when they were ready. Manny was going to meet up with Mona later at the country club. He was going to spend the morning helping his mom with Glen and Poppie.

Mona had brought her dress along to change into before going to the country club. All of the bridesmaids were going to change at Charise's. Charise was going to change at the country club. There was a room set aside for her use.

As soon as Mona arrived, she got her tools out and went to work. She started on hair. Gloria was first. She had flown home for the wedding. Barton returned with her. He was staying at Fitness Central in the storm shelter.

Mona quickly finished with Gloria and went on to Sylvia and Hallie. Mona showed Gloria how to do the makeup and had her working on Sylvia while she finished up with Hallie. The girls went on to get dressed as soon as Mona was finished with them. Mona got busy with Babs and Evone next. Gloria went to get dressed, and Hallie volunteered to help with makeup. Mona had fixed her hair and makeup before she came. All she had to do to be ready was put on her dress and shoes.

After finishing with the others, Mona had Charise sit down and went to work on her. She fixed her hair first. Charise had shown her a picture of the hairstyle she wanted. It was an old-fashioned hairstyle with an upsweep and a roll. Mona worked on her hair, and it was turning out perfectly. The girls all stood around, watching in awe.

"You are an artist," declared Sylvia as she watched Charise's hairstyle develop.

Mona grinned. "Thanks, I love working with hair. I don't usually get a chance to do any fancy work. Most ladies want something easy to take care of."

Mona finished with Charise's hair and makeup and left her to get dressed. The bridesmaids were using Gloria's room to get dressed in. The other girls were helping Charise, so Mona had the room to herself. She quickly slipped into her dress. She touched up her makeup and checked her hair and went to see if any more help was needed with the other girls.

Charise was putting on all of her clothes except her dress. She was wearing a robe and carrying the bag with her dress in it.

They were all ready by twelve-thirty, and the limo was waiting out front of her house. They had made arrangements for the limo to drop them off at a side door. It led directly into their dressing room. The men had a dressing room on the other side of the building close to the flower-covered alter.

The photographer was going around taking pictures. He took several pictures of the girls as they entered and went to the bride's room. Charise's mother and father were there.

They were anxiously awaiting the arrival of Senator and Mrs. Willis and Governor and Mrs. Hayes. They were arriving together with their security teams. They were all flying in on Senator Willis' private plane. Mrs. Willis and Mrs. Hayes were friends, also. They were all originally from Rolling Fork. They had all moved to the capital some time ago as their husbands committed to government service. Mrs. Willis was looking forward to her husband's retirement and their move to Sharpville. She wanted to be close to Zachery and Charise and any possible grandchildren.

"Hello, Love," thought Manny.

"Hello, are you here?" thought Mona.

"Yes, I just arrived. They are seating me on the brides' side," thought Manny.

"I'm glad you are here. We shouldn't have but another thirty minutes before starting," thought Mona.

"I'm enjoying people watching. I think the Governor and Senator have arrived. There is security everywhere," thought Manny.

"How exciting, let me tell Charise. I love you," thought Mona.

Mona smiled to herself as she turned to let Charise know her future in-laws had arrived. "The Senator and Governor are arriving," said Mona.

Charise smiled. It was almost time for her to become Mrs. Zachery Willis.

Hallie and Babs went down the hall to see if they could get a glimpse of Governor Hayes and Senator Willis. Gloria went to an *en suite* refrigerator and removed the flower bouquets that they would all be carrying down the aisle. There were small bouquets for each girl and a large bridal bouquet for Charise. There were flower corsages for the bride and groom's mothers. The flowers for the groomsmen were in the groom's dressing room. There were also flowers for the groom and his father.

"There are three corsages in here," said Gloria.

"Mother probably included one for Mrs. Hayes," said Charise. "Gloria, why don't you take them to Mother so she can give them to Mrs. Willis and Mrs. Hayes?"

"Okay," agreed Gloria. She scooped up the three corsages and went to give them to her mother.

Charise had put on her dress, and Mona was checking her hair and makeup to see if they were in need of touch-ups.

There was a knock at the door. When Mona opened the door Charise's dad was there. "Is Charise ready? They are about ready to start playing the music," he said.

"I'm ready," said Charise. "Tell the girls to come and line up for the march," Charise told Mona.

Mona left to round up the bridesmaids and Hallie, the matron of honor. She met them on their way back to the room. She gave them the message and went on to find Gloria.

She found Gloria down the aisle, helping the ladies pin on their corsages. She gave her the message and, when she turned to return to the back, she spotted Manny. He was smiling at her. She smiled back and reached over to squeeze his hand when she was close to where he was sitting.

"You look beautiful," said Manny softly.

"You look handsome," said Mona giving him a quick once over.

Mona reluctantly released his hand and continued on to the back. Several of the security guards gave her a once over and a smile as she passed them. Mona smiled back but didn't stop.

Gloria caught up with her just before she arrived at the bride's room.

Gloria smiled at Mona. "I had to say hello to Barton. He was sitting with Manny," said Gloria.

"I didn't notice," said Mona.

Gloria smiled. "You only saw Manny," she remarked.

"Yeah," agreed Mona as they entered the bride's room.

"Good, everyone is here. Babs, you go first, Mona can follow you and Gloria can follow her. Since you two were not at the rehearsal, all you have to do is follow Babs and do what she does," said Charise.

The music started and the girls lined up in the hall to start the march down the aisle. Mona watched Babs closely until she got to the front, and then she copied her movements as she made her way to the beginning of the aisle. Gloria followed as Mona came to a stop beside Babs.

They waited patiently while the others followed them down the aisle. After Hallie made it down, the music changed, and everyone stood for the bride and her father to make their way down the aisle. After Larry Harris placed Charise's hand in Zachery's, he made his way over and sat beside his wife Delilah.

Zachery smiled at Charise. "You look beautiful," he whispered.

"Thanks," said Charise smiling back at him.

The preacher started the service. Most people paid very little attention to his words. They were too busy trying to get a good look at the Governor and Senator. Governor Hayes watched with satisfaction as his Godson made a commitment to this lovely girl. They were perfect together, he thought. They reminded him of when he and Mrs. Hayes were just starting their lives together.

Senator and Mrs. Willis were also happily watching Zachery and Charise take their vows. They were happy

Zachery was getting out of the Navy Seals and taking a less dangerous approach to life.

The preacher had them repeat their vows and exchange rings. "You may kiss the bride," said the preacher.

"With pleasure," said Zachery as he followed the preacher's directions.

"May I present Mr. and Mrs. Zachery Willis," said the preacher.

Charise and Zachery turned to face an applauding audience as they started and back down the aisle. The bridesmaids and groomsmen followed them out. They did not have far to go. The country club had set up a room next door for the continuing celebration.

The band was playing, and the cake was in a place of honor. Zachery and Charise stopped just inside the door and waited to greet Senator and Mrs. Willis and Governor and Mrs. Hayes.

Mona stopped in the hall to wait for Manny. Manny and Barton came out together. Manny hurried to Mona's side and hugged her. Gloria appeared to claim Barton. After they hugged, Mona greeted Barton and apologized for not noticing him before.

Barton grinned at her. "That's okay, I was watching Gloria. She looks so beautiful."

Gloria gave him another hug and the two couples headed into the room with the rest of the guests.

Charise and Zachery were still talking to the Senator and the Governor and their wives just inside the door. When Gloria and Barton entered with Mona and Manny just behind them, Charise drew them to a stop to introduce them.

"This is my sister, Gloria and her boyfriend Barton Evans," said Charise.

"Ah, the veterinarian students," said Governor Hayes.

"It's a pleasure to meet you. I hear you both are doing very well in school."

"Thank you, Sir," said Barton. Gloria barely managed to say hello. She was astonished to hear the Governor talk so casually about them.

Barton drew Gloria away to dance, and Charise drew Mona forward. "This is Mona Santoes and Manny McCray. They are engaged, and Mona did the hair and makeup for all of us. We really appreciate it, as her mom is in the hospital," said Charise.

"You do beautiful work," said Mrs. Hayes. "I have been admiring Charise's hair. It looks beautiful."

"Yes, it does," agreed Mrs. Willis. "I hope your mom will be alright."

"Thank you," said Mona. "We are all praying for her."

"It is nice to meet you all," said Manny. He drew Mona away into the room where they could circulate and greet people.

"Is her mom going to be alright?" asked Mrs. Willis.

"We don't know," said Zachery. "She is in a coma and has to have brain surgery."

It was a very somber group who made their way on into the room. They took their seats at the main table. They made sure their guests were in seats of honor. The security guards were scattered around the room keeping an eye out for trouble.

Gloria and Barton took their seats after they finished their dance. Gloria was glad her mother and father were preoccupied with their special guests and were not paying any attention to her and Barton. Manny drew Mona over and seated her at the table so they could toast the bride and groom.

Since Joey was the best man, he was standing waiting for everyone to get a glass so he could give a toast to the newlyweds. "Everyone raise your glass and let us toast the magic mirror," said Joey. "It has had a profound effect on our lives, and it has shown a lot of us the way to true love. To Zachery and Charise, may they always be as in love as they are today and may we all bask in the glow of their love."

"Hear, hear," agreed the crowd.

"Thank you, Joey. A different toast but very true," said Zachery. "I am very happy the magic mirror showed me to Charise and started us on the journey to each other. I promise Charise I will never let her or the magic mirror down."

Charise watched as Mona and Manny slipped out. She knew they were on the way to check on her mom. Charise stood up. She waited until she had everyone's attention before talking.

"I am happy with my new life with Zachery, but I want to talk to you about something else. My friend Mona has left to return to the hospital. Her mom is in a coma. She has a tumor on her brain stem and will be operated on this next Tuesday. She needs all of our prayers. She also needs blood. If any of you are type B or O, please go to the Sharpville hospital and donate to Jewel Santoes. Even if you aren't B or O, any donations made to Jewel Santoes could help with the costs of surgery. Zachery and I are going to stop and donate on our way to the airport before going on our honeymoon. So, while we loved having you all here to celebrate with us, we are going to leave now. If you ladies will pack up our cake and give it to my parents, we will have a party when we return and cut it then. Thank you all for coming."

Charise took Zachery's hand and they made their way out saying goodbyes. Some of their friends followed them out.

Governor Hayes looked at Senator Willis. "What blood type are you?" he asked.

"Type B, what type are you?" asked Senator Willis.

"Type B," said the Governor. "Does anyone know the way to this hospital?"

The security guard, standing behind the Governor, leaned forward. "It's in the town where we left the airplane," he said.

Governor Hayes rose and helped his wife to stand. Senator Willis helped Mrs. Willis to stand also. The security guards led the way and surrounded them as they went out to their limo. Joey and Hallie followed them out.

"If you will follow me, I will show you the way to the hospital," said Joey.

"Are you going to donate?" asked Governor Hayes.

"Hallie and I have already donated," said Joey.

The governor nodded. "Thank you, we will be right behind you."

Joey and Hallie got into their car and pulled around front to wait for the limo. The security guard signaled they were ready to go. Joey pulled out and led the way to Sharpville and the hospital; there were three cars behind him. The first car had security. The second car has the Governor and the Senator and their wives. The third car was also security. They made good time going to Sharpville and on to the hospital. Everyone who saw them pulled over and waited until they passed.

Hallie laughed. "There is no way I expected this when I got ready for the wedding this morning," she said.

Joey grinned. "Life is full of surprises," said Joey.

Joey pulled under the covered walkway at the hospital. He pulled on through so the car in the middle would be right in front of the door. Joey pulled into a parking space, and he and Hallie went to show the way to the blood donor lab. The security teams from both men checked around to be sure there was no danger as they went toward the lab.

Joey and Hallie went back out into the hall, so the room

would not be so crowded. Zachery and Charise came out of another door while they were waiting.

Zachery looked surprised to see them. "I thought you had already donated."

"We did. We came to show the governor and the senator the way to the hospital," said Hallie.

"Dad and Uncle Ralph are here?" said Zachery.

"Yes, they are donating. Both are type B," said Joey.

Zachery grinned. "I bet they didn't think this was going to happen when they decided to come to our wedding," said Zachery.

A couple of security guards came out and went down the hall. They both nodded and spoke to Zachery. He smiled and spoke back. Governor Hayes and Senator Willis came out. Zachery grinned at them and looked around. "Where is Mom," he asked.

"She and Mrs. Hayes decided to donate, too," said Senator Willis.

"Some of the security guards are taking turns donating, also," said Governor Hayes. "Would you happen to know where the business office is?"

"Yes, sir, I can show you where it is," said Charise. "I have done some volunteer work here," she said. Charise started out holding tight to Zachery's hand. The others followed her along with two security guards. Charise had removed her veil in the limo, but she was still wearing her wedding dress.

When they reached the business office the Governor and the Senator went in. The others waited, watching through the window. They saw the two take out their checkbooks and write out checks to help with Jewel's medical expenses.

When they came out of the office, they looked very pleased with themselves. They went back to the donor room to find their wives waiting for them, and the security guards were also done. They all started out the front door of the hospital. When they came out, a camera flashed as a reporter took a picture of them.

"Could you tell us why you are at our hospital, Sir?" the reporter asked the Governor.

"We were here donating blood and setting up a fund for a friend of my Godson. She has to have brain surgery and is in need of type B blood and help with expenses," said Governor Hayes. "Tell your readers to send any donations to the hospital marked for Jewel Santoes. Any help will be greatly appreciated." They all climbed into their cars and left while the reporter scrambled to report the biggest scoop of his career.

Joey and Hallie bid Zachery and Charise goodbye and headed for Fitness Central. Zachery and Charise followed the other cars to the airport. Zachery and Charise went to catch their private plane to start their honeymoon. Charise had her clothes waiting on their plane, so she could change out of her wedding dress.

The others headed for Senator Willis' plane and the trip back to the capital.

CHAPTER 11

*U*naware of the drama going on a few floors below them, Mona and Manny had managed to get Giles to take a break and let Mona sit with her mom for a while. Manny handed Giles the coffee and sandwich they had picked up on their way to the hospital.

Giles drank the coffee and nibbled on the sandwich. He laid the sandwich on a table in the waiting room. After taking another swallow of coffee, he looked at Manny.

"How did the wedding go?" he asked.

"It was going along fine when we left," said Manny.

"Did the Governor really show up?" asked Giles.

"Yes, he was there. Between the two of them, there was quite a group of security guards," said Manny.

Giles laughed. "Barons will be talking about it for years to come," he observed.

Manny smiled. "I imagine they will. Charise has promised Mona copies of pictures so she can show them to her mom when she is better."

"Jewel will like that," said Giles. "She will be the star of the Cut and Curl. How are the kids doing? Are they behaving themselves?"

"They are fine. I think they both like being at the ranch. Glen had his first riding lesson. He did very well. He was calm and in control," said Manny. "Mom was giving Poppie a cooking lesson this morning. They both seemed to be enjoying the lesson."

"Good," said Giles. "It will help to keep them busy so they don't worry about their mom so much."

"If it's alright with you, I would like to continue Glen's riding lessons after Mona and I are married," said Manny.

"It's fine with me. Glen will love it. He has always been crazy about horses." said Giles.

"He is very good with them. He has a feel for them and how to act around them," said Manny.

"Have you heard how Beth is doing?" asked Giles.

"I haven't heard since we went by, but I'm sure she is okay. She promised to help Erin clean her room," said Manny.

Giles laughed. "Beth hates cleaning her room. It will be a real challenge for her and Erin. Maybe it won't be so bad since they will be working together," said Giles. Giles lay his head against the chair back and closed his eyes.

"Why don't you go home and stretch out for a few hours and get a good sleep? Mona and I will be here; and, after the operation, you may not be able to get away for a few days," said Manny.

Giles sat up straight and looked at Manny. "You may be right. I think I will go and try to get some sleep."

Manny stood up when Giles stood. "Are you sure you are alright to drive?" he asked.

"I'll be fine. Tell Mona I'll be back after I get some sleep," said Giles.

"I'll tell her. We will call you if there is any change, but there is not likely to be any change as long as they keep Jewel in a coma," said Manny.

"I know," said Giles. "Thanks for looking after my family."

"You are all my family, too. Mona and I are going to be married as soon as her mom can attend a wedding," said Manny. Giles just smiled and left to go home.

When Giles was leaving the hospital to go home, he saw the caravan of cars pull out and head away. He didn't pay any attention to it. He headed for his car. He had other things on his mind.

"Hello, Love," thought Mona.

"Hi, are you okay?" thought Manny.

"I'm fine. How is Giles doing?" thought Mona.

"I talked him into going home and getting some sleep. I told him we would stay and call him if anything happened," thought Manny.

"Good. He needed to stretch out and sleep," thought Mona. "Do you want to go on home and come back to pick me up later?"

"I'm not going anywhere, and I am not going to leave you here by yourself," thought Manny.

"I love you. The doctor just came in. Let me see what he has to say," thought Mona.

"How is she doing?" Mona asked the doctor.

"There is no change. It is good news. She is stable; as long as she stays stable, she will do better in an operation," said the doctor.

"Is she still scheduled for Tuesday?" asked Mona.

"Yes, the surgeon is supposed to be here Monday night so he can study the case and be ready for Tuesday morning," said the doctor. "Is your young man still waiting for you in the waiting room?"

"Yes, he managed to get my stepdad to go home and get some sleep," said Mona.

The doctor looked thoughtful. "Your mom is in a private room. I see no reason why your young man couldn't come in and sit with you while you wait."

Mona smiled at the doctor. "Thank you, doctor. It will make waiting much easier if I have someone waiting with me," said Mona.

"I'll go by on my way out and tell him he can come in," said the doctor as he left.

A few minutes later, Manny came through the door. He was smiling as he entered. Mona hurried over to him and hugged him tight. When she let him go, Manny led her to the chair by the bed and moved another chair by her so he could hold her hand while they waited.

"Mom, this is Manny." Mona squeezed her mom's hand. "He is going to be your son-in-law. We are only waiting until you are better to be married. You are going to love him. He is a wonderful person." She smiled at Manny before continuing talking to her mom. "He makes me happy, and the kids love him, too, especially Glen. He is caring and smart and an all-around good guy. I can't wait for you to get to know him."

Manny gave her shoulder a squeeze. "Hello, Mrs. Santoes, I am sorry we have to meet under these circumstances. I love your daughter with all of my heart. She is my heart." Mona smiled at him and squeezed his hand. "I am going to make it my life's goal to be sure she never regrets being my wife. Glen is a great little boy. It is a pleasure to have him around and teach him to ride. I hope Mona and I have a son or daughter just like him someday. You are a very lucky woman. Giles is devoted to you, and you have four wonderful children. Soon, you will be well, and you will understand what a lucky person you are to be surrounded by so much love."

Mona squeezed his hand again and looked at him misty-eyed. "I love you," said Manny.

"I love you, too," said Mona.

Mona leaned her head on his shoulder, and they sat quietly enjoying the closeness for a while. Mona watched her mom, lying there so peaceful. Even though she was hooked up to the machines, she looked like she was pain free and at peace. It had been a long time since Mona had seen her mom without pain.

Surely this operation would solve her problems and get rid of the pain. She could get back to enjoying her life and her family. It would be a great relief on all of them. They all had felt the effects of her illness. It would make a huge difference for Beth, Poppie, and Glen, but Giles would be the most relieved. He had been so worried. Jewel was the love of his life. Mona understood that better since she had fallen in love with Manny.

Manny held her close and Mona laid her head on his chest. Her eyes closed and she dozed off. Manny eased them both into a more comfortable position and held her close, as she had a much-needed nap.

The nurse came in to check on Jewel, but when she saw Mona sleeping, she was very quiet while she checked. She gave Manny a smile as she left. He smiled back but didn't say anything. He didn't want to chance waking Mona.

When Giles reached home, he took a shower and then lay down and was asleep almost before his head touched the pillow.

At the McCray ranch, they were sampling the cookies Poppie and Cathy had made. Poppie was glowing in the praise heaped on her as the cookies disappeared. They all took their cookies into the living room with glasses of milk, and Alvin put on a movie for them to watch while they enjoyed their snack. Glen and Poppie sat on bean bags and Cathy and Alvin sat on the sofa. Alvin put his arm around Cathy and held her close as they enjoyed having young people in the house again.

It was sometime later when Mona stirred and opened her eyes. She sat up straight and looked at Manny. "I'm sorry, I didn't mean to pass out on you," she said.

Manny smiled and kissed her lightly. "I'm glad I was able to be here for you. You are worn out. The rest will help, but when this is over, I wouldn't be surprised if you slept the clock around."

"I wouldn't mind, if I could sleep in your arms," said Mona kissing him lightly.

The door opened and the nurse came in. She smiled at Mona as she went to check on Jewel. "I am glad to see you had a nice nap," she said.

"Yes, I feel much better," said Mona. "Having Manny close helped a lot."

The nurse smiled. "I wouldn't mind finding a guy like him to hold me while I sleep," she said.

"Have you been to Danny's to look in the magic mirror?" asked Mona.

The nurse looked at her startled. "You mean you saw him in the magic mirror?"

Mona and Manny both nodded. They had large grins on their faces. "Yes, we met through the magic mirror," said Mona.

"Well, I'll be. I'm going in there first chance I get," said the nurse. "We had a bit of excitement here earlier. The Governor and Senator stopped by to donate blood for your mother. They also put money into a fund to help with costs of the operation."

Mona sat up straight. "They donated blood and money for Mom?"

"Yes, there was quite a crowd downstairs. It is the talk of the hospital," said the nurse with a grin.

Mona looked at Manny. Manny shook his head. "I didn't know anything about it. Charise and Zachery must have asked them, before they left on their honeymoon."

Mona grinned. "Mom is going to be over the moon when she finds out whose blood she is getting."

"I'll see you later," said the nurse as she left with a smile.

Mona took her mom's hand and gave it a small squeeze. "Did you hear that, Mom? You are going to be famous in Barons and at the Cut and Curl. The Governor and Senator Willis donated blood for you. I'm going to have to send both of them thank you notes," said Mona.

"I think it would be best to wait and let your mom send notes when she is better. She will love being able to write and thank them herself," said Manny.

"You are right," agreed Mona. "I am so used to taking care of things. I tend to take over sometimes."

"You can take over my life anytime you want to," said Manny. "It is wonderful to have you here in my arms. Everything else we can work out later."

"Yes, later," agreed Mona as she kissed him.

"Would you like for me to go and get you some coffee?" asked Manny.

"No, I don't want you to leave. I love being here with your arms around me. I can wait and we will stop and eat when Giles gets back," said Mona.

"I like having you in my arms, too," said Manny. "I am looking forward to many years of having you in my arms, but not in a hospital, in our home and in our bed."

"I can't wait," said Mona, kissing him again.

Manny's phone buzzed. He took it out and looked at it. "It's Mom. I forgot to turn it off when I came in here," said Manny.

"Hello, Mom, I can't talk long. I'm not supposed to have my phone on in here," said Manny.

"Okay, I won't keep you. I just wanted to let you know there was a story about the Governor and Senator donating blood and money on the news this morning," said Cathy.

"I knew about the donations. I didn't know it was on the news. Thanks for letting me know," said Manny.

"Let me know if we can help. Give Mona our love," said Cathy.

"I will. Bye, Mom," said Manny.

"Mom said the news told the story about the Governor and Senator Willis making donations for your mom," said Manny.

"Oh my, I can't believe this," said Mona.

"It will be fine. I know it doesn't seem like it sometimes, but there are a lot of good people in the world. They still believe in helping when they can," said Manny.

"I know, everyone has been very helpful since Mom has been sick. It really shows a person how many friends they have when something like this happens," said Mona.

"Yes, it can also make you a bunch of new friends," agreed Manny.

The door opened and Giles came in. "Did you get some rest?" asked Mona, going over to give him a hug.

"Yes, thanks, I feel much better," said Giles. He looked surprised to see Manny there with Mona.

"The doctor said Manny could stay in here with me. He said since Mom's room is private, we wouldn't be disturbing anyone," said Mona.

Giles smiled and nodded at Manny. "I'm glad you could stay with Mona," he said. Manny smiled and nodded at him.

"Did you hear about the Governor and the Senator donating blood for Mom?' asked Mona.

"Yes, one of the nurses stopped me on the way in. It seems the business office has been flooded with donations to help with the cost of the operation and any other expenses," said Giles.

"Wow," said Mona.

"Why don't you two take off and get something to eat and get some rest," said Giles. "Thanks for staying, so I could rest."

He looked at Manny as he said the last part. Manny smiled and nodded. He took Mona's hand to leave.

"We will see you later. Let us know if you need us," said Mona as she and Manny left.

As they went down the hall to the elevator, there was an air of suppressed excitement as they passed the nurses at the desk.

There were news people around the front door, but as they did not know who Mona and Manny were, they were able to leave without any trouble.

CHAPTER 12

Manny and Mona stopped at a pancake house and ate before going on home. They went to the McCray ranch. Cathy and Alvin had taken Poppie and Glen to church, so there was no one home. Mona and Manny went to shower and change clothes. They met in the living room when they finished dressing.

Manny took Mona's hand and led her to the sofa. He sat down and pulled her down beside him so he could hold her in his arms.

"Aren't you sleepy?" asked Mona.

"A little, but I want to hold you in my arms more than I want to sleep," answered Manny.

Manny reached for the remote and turned the television on. He turned the sound down some. He mainly wanted background noise.

The news was on. Manny and Mona watched as the reporter showed Governor Hayes and Mrs. Hayes along with Senator and Mrs. Willis leaving the hospital accompanied by their security guards. The reporter went on to tell about the donations and how help was needed for Jewel Santoes.

Mona couldn't believe her family was in the news this way. They had always seemed to be in the background. This put the spotlight directly on them. The news reporter had even found out about Jewel working at the Cut and Curl. They had interviewed Pat and some of the other ladies working there. Hazel really enjoyed being in the spotlight; she even mentioned Mona and Manny.

"She just doesn't know when to shut up," observed Mona.

Manny laughed. "I don't mind being known as your boy toy," he remarked. "It looks like your boss lady has shut her up." Mona and Manny watched as Pat drew the reporter's attention away from Hazel and back to herself. She gave Hazel a stern look that sent her back to work.

The reporter switched his attention away from the Cut and Curl and back to the hospital. They showed the Governor's caravan leaving the hospital the day before, after making their donations.

They finally switched to other news, and Mona looked at Manny and grinned. "Mom's going to be sorry she missed all of the excitement. She loves to be in the middle of things. All of this is going on around her, and she is out of it."

"I'm sure the news will be repeated over again when she wakes up. She will get to see it then," said Manny.

Poppie followed Glen in the door with Cathy and Alvin following. Glen ran over to hug Mona and Manny as soon as he saw them. Poppie came more slowly, but she also hugged Mona. She looked at Manny undecided until he opened his arms and then she hugged him also. Mona and Manny smiled at each other over Poppie's head.

"How is your mom?" asked Cathy as she came over and hugged Mona also.

"She is the same. The doctor said it was good for her to

remain stable. It will make the operation go smoother," said Mona.

"Did you see about the Governor on the news?" asked Poppie excitedly.

Mona grinned. "Manny and I were just watching it," said Mona.

"They showed it again?" asked Poppie.

"I imagine they will show it quite a few times," said Cathy. "It is big news for our small town. Sharpville is larger, but they don't have the Governor visiting very often."

"I don't remember him ever visiting," said Alvin. "He may have come through when he was campaigning for office."

"It was nice of him to help out," said Cathy.

"I think he is a nice guy and he helps when something is brought to his attention. We may be hearing more from him now since Zachery is making his home here. He seems to be very hands on Godfather," said Mona.

"Senator Willis is planning on building a house around here for when he retires," said Manny. "I overheard some people talking about it."

"He and Mrs. Willis probably want to be close to their future grandchildren," said Cathy.

"I'm sure they are taking that into consideration," said Manny.

"Have any of you talked to Beth?" asked Mona.

"I talked to her," said Poppie. "She wanted to know if we had heard anything. I told her you were spending a lot of time at the hospital, and there was no change. She said they finished cleaning Erin's room, and Erin's mom took them out for ice cream as a thank you."

"I'll talk to her before I go back to the hospital," said Mona.

"Your dad was asking about you all earlier," said Manny.

"He wanted to know how you were all doing. I told him you were all worried about your mom, but you were doing the best you could to be brave until you have good news."

"When you go back to the hospital, could you tell Dad we love him and we are praying for Mom?" said Poppie.

"I will give him your message," promised Manny.

"You two need to go and change your clothes so you can eat," said Mona. Poppie and Glen quickly left to go and change. "Can I help you with lunch?" Mona asked Cathy.

"You can help me set the table. I left a stew cooking in the crockpot," said Cathy.

Mona followed Cathy into the kitchen. "It smells delicious," said Mona, taking a deep breath.

Cathy laughed. "I love having a crockpot. It makes preparing a lunch when you are not home a lot easier. Just let me pop some loaves of bread into the oven. While it is cooking, we can make drinks and put out bowls."

Mona put bowls and spoons out and filled glasses with iced tea. She put the glasses on the table but left the bowls on the cabinet to be filled with stew.

Manny and Alvin were in the living room, talking quietly. Alvin was catching Manny up on ranch business he had missed while being with Mona at the hospital.

Poppie and Glen came back down. Poppie came to the kitchen to see if she could help. Glen joined the guys in the living room. Mona looked toward the living room and glanced around the kitchen. She stood up straight and, putting her hands on her hips, looked at Cathy.

"They learn early, don't they," said Mona.

Cathy laughed. "I think they sense that they just get in our way in the kitchen. They know we are organized and get irritated when they don't do things the way we want them done," said Cathy.

Mona grinned. "You may be right. It is still irritating," she said.

"I know," agreed Cathy.

Poppie looked from one to the other. She didn't understand what they were talking about.

Cathy took the bread out and sliced it and set it on the table.

Mona took the ladle and filled the bowls with stew. She and Poppie carefully put them on the table.

"Poppie, why don't you tell the gentlemen in the living room that lunch is ready," said Cathy. "I have chocolate cake for dessert. I'll leave it on the counter to be served later."

"It smells great," said Mona. "Everyone will be in a hurry to finish their stew so they can get to the cake."

Cathy laughed. "I have found the food disappears faster if they can smell dessert."

"Good thinking," said Mona with a laugh. "I'll have to remember that."

The guys came into the dining room and settled around the table. They all held hands as Alvin said the blessing and added a wish for Jewel to do well in her operation. Mona smiled a thank you at him when he finished.

"This smells great, Mom," said Manny. Mona grinned and glanced at Cathy when she caught him glancing at the chocolate cake on the counter. Cathy smiled back at her, but she continued eating as if she hadn't noticed anything.

After they had all finished their stew in record time, Mona and Cathy went to serve the cake. Cathy cut the cake and Mona passed it around to everyone before sitting and digging into her own. Everyone was eating the cake with blissful expressions on their faces. It was easy to see the cake was a McCray family favorite.

After they finished eating, Poppie and Glen helped clear

the table. They took the dishes into the kitchen where Cathy rinsed them and put them into the dishwasher.

Mona and Manny went to lie down and try to sleep for a while. They were planning to go back to the hospital and sit with Jewel while Giles got some rest. Before she lay down, Mona called Beth and talked to her for a bit. She didn't talk long; she was too sleepy. Mona started to try to talk to Manny, but she was afraid she would keep him awake and he needed to sleep. Mona closed her eyes and was soon fast asleep.

Alvin took Glen and Poppie for a walk down to the pasture so they could see the horses. They stood at the fence and gazed in wonder as the mares with new babies frolicked around and played. Glen had brought some sugar cubes with him to try and feed the horses. He had watched Manny do it and he wanted to try.

Alvin whistled for the horses and a couple of them, with their babies, came over to investigate. Glen held his hand out flat with a sugar cube on it. He stood very still and smiled up at Alvin as one of the mares delicately took the sugar cube off of his hand. He put another cube on his hand and held it out. This time, when the mare was taking the cube, Glen rubbed his other hand between her eyes and down her nose. The mare pushed her nose into Glen's hand, and he laughed delightedly.

Alvin smiled indulgently. He remembered when his boys had been so young and full of wonder. They loved feeding the mares sugar cubes too. They just made sure their grandfather was not around when they did. It was a blessing Amos McCray was no longer interested in the ranch since he began palling around with Sebastian Kantor. It sure made life much happier for the rest of them.

Alvin took Poppie and Glen by the smokehouse. This was where they smoked and cured the meat for their own use.

"Ohhh, this smells good," said Poppie when Alvin opened the door to the smokehouse.

"Yes, it does," agreed Glen.

"It was always a favorite of my boys. They love coming here and getting some meat to take out with them when they had to work out on the ranch," said Alvin.

He took out his knife. After wiping it off on his handkerchief, Alvin sliced a small piece of meat for Poppie and one for Glen.

"Is it alright to eat it without cooking it?" asked Poppie.

"It has been fully cured. It is safe to eat," said Alvin with a smile.

Glen was already eating his piece. "This is good, Poppie," said Glen.

Poppie took a small bite then smiled at Alvin and Glen. "It is great," agreed Poppie.

They went out, and Alvin carefully closed and turned the latch on the door. "We don't want any animals getting in and eating all of our meat," said Alvin.

They started back toward the house. When they went in, the kids hurried over to Cathy, who was resting on the sofa and doing some needlework. Glen excitedly told her about feeding sugar cubes to the mares. Poppie told her about eating meat without cooking it.

Cathy laughed. "It sounds like you two have been enjoying yourselves," said Cathy. "Help yourself to some Kool-Aid to wash down the meat you ate."

They had Kool-Aid packets with straws in them for the kids. The kids loved them, and it cut down on washing glasses.

Alvin sat down next to Cathy on the sofa. Cathy looked up at him and smiled before going back to her needlework. "It is so nice to see the wonder on little faces as they discover things for the first time," said Alvin.

"Yes, I was watching Poppie's face when she was learning to make cookies. It was wonderful," said Cathy. "They are so happy to be learning. I hope we will have a chance to have them over after this medical crisis is over."

Alvin reached for the TV remote and turned the TV on and started looking to see what was on. "Did Manny and Mona say when they were going back to the hospital?" asked Alvin.

"No, I didn't ask. I wanted them to get as much sleep as they could. They have really been pushing their selves the last few days, and it's not going to get any better for a few days after the operation," said Cathy

Poppie and Glen came back into the room and sat down to watch TV with them while they drank their Kool-Aid. Alvin found a child-friendly show, and they all settled back to watch it.

They had watched a couple of shows before Mona and Manny made an appearance. They had both showered and dressed to go back to the hospital.

"I have you both a plate fixed. They are in the oven," said Cathy.

Mona and Manny headed for the kitchen. They knew better than to argue with Cathy. Besides, they knew they needed to eat before going back to the hospital.

Cathy followed them into the kitchen. They were sitting at the counter eating. "I fixed a plate for your stepdad also. He needs some good food. I also put in a large slice of my chocolate cake," said Cathy.

"We will take it to him. You are spoiling us," said Mona.

"You are going to be my daughter," said Cathy. "I want to be sure you are okay."

"Thank you," said Mona, smiling at Cathy while she squeezed Manny's hand.

Manny squeezed her hand back and smiled at her. "Did you save us a slice of the chocolate cake?" asked Manny.

Cathy went to the refrigerator and brought out two slices of chocolate cake and placed them in front of Manny and Mona.

Manny leaned over and kissed her cheek. "Thanks, Mom. You are the best," said Manny.

Cathy smiled and shook her head. "You will let us know if there is anything we can do," said Cathy.

"Not having to worry about Poppie and Glen is a blessing. You and Alvin are helping a lot," said Mona.

"I've loved having them here," said Cathy. "Alvin loves having them here, too. He took them for a walk this afternoon. He introduced them to our smokehouse. I remember how you boys used to slip in there," said Cathy.

"Yes," said Manny laughing. "We almost got caught a few times by Granddad. Dad covered for us and helped us slip away."

"He liked slipping in there as much as you boys did," said Cathy with a smile.

"You mean Dad slipped in there, too," said Manny.

"Of course he did. He loves the taste of the meat fresh from the smokehouse," said Cathy. "I promised I wouldn't give him away if he slipped me a slice, also."

"It is your smokehouse," said Mona. "Why couldn't you just go and get meat whenever you wanted to?"

Cathy laughed. "It was much more fun our way," she said.

Mona shook her head. "It was all a game. You were enjoying slipping the meat past everyone."

"Yes," agreed Cathy. "It was a fun game."

Mona just smiled and turned to Manny. "We need to go," she said.

"Thanks for the meal, Cathy," said Mona as they rose

from their stools and took their plates to the sink. They rinsed the plates and put them in the dishwasher.

"Thanks, Mom," said Manny as they came back by Cathy. He kissed her on the cheek again.

"You are both welcome," said Cathy. "Drive carefully."

"We will," promised Manny.

CHAPTER 13

*W*hen they arrived at the hospital, they met Arnold Payne at the door He was going in at the same time they were. Mona looked at him in surprise.

"Hello, Arnold. What are you doing here? Is Mary Ellen and the baby okay?" she asked.

"They are fine," said Arnold. He flushed slightly as he faced Mona. "I was stopping by to deliver a donation for your mom's medical fund. Dad asked me to bring it by for him, and I wanted to donate, too."

Mona was shaking her head. "It's fine for you to deliver your dad's donation, but you and Mary Ellen need your money for your baby. You can buy baby furniture or diapers and clothes. If you don't need it for those things, open a trust fund for the baby's future. My mom has had a lot of money donated for her medical expenses. I don't know how much, but if it isn't enough, we will manage. You and Mary Ellen are just getting started, and you need the money." said Mona.

Arnold was looking at her startled. Manny was grinning at her. He was so very proud of her.

Mona looked at Manny. "Do you two know each other?' she asked.

Arnold shook his head. "I have seen you around, but you were out of school before me, so we didn't really get acquainted.

Manny nodded. "We didn't run in the same groups," he agreed.

"Well, Arnold, this is my fiancé Manny McCray. Manny, this is Charise's former fiancé," said Mona.

"It's nice to meet you," said Manny, holding his hand out to shake Arnold's."

Arnold shook his hand. "Mona, do you suppose you could find another way to introduce me? I'm sure I will live it down someday if we don't mention it."

Mona laughed. "I'm sorry. I don't suppose Mary Ellen would like it too much either," said Mona. "When is the baby due?"

Arnold smiled. "We have about three more months," he said.

"Well, if either of you need anything, let me know. If you are in need of Godparents, keep Manny and me in mind."

"I think you and Manny would make great Godparents. I'll talk it over with Mary Ellen and let you know, thanks," said Arnold.

"We need to get upstairs. We will see you later," said Mona.

Manny and Arnold said goodbye, and Arnold headed for the office. He took Mona's words to heart and donated his dad's check and took his with him to open an account for baby Payne at the bank in Barons the next day.

Manny and Mona went on upstairs. In the elevator, Mona looked at Manny. "You don't mind me volunteering us for Godparents, do you? I should have asked you first."

Manny pulled her close in his arms. "I love kids. If Arnold does decide to ask us to be Godparents, it will be my pleasure to be one. Just ask me first next time," Manny teased, kissing her.

"I will, I promise," said Mona as the doors opened on their floor.

They went down to Jewel's room and entered. They found Giles sitting in a chair by her bed, holding her hand and talking to her.

Giles looked up as they entered and smiled at them.

Manny took the food Cathy had sent over to Giles and set it on the table. "Mom was worried you were not getting enough to eat, so she sent you a plate and dessert," said Manny.

Giles sniffed and smiled. "It smells great. Please thank her for me."

"Has there been any news from the doctor?" asked Mona.

"No, everything is still set for Tuesday morning," said Giles.

"Why don't you take your food and go home and get some sleep. Manny and I will stay here with Mom. We both had a good sleep today, and you need to sleep," said Mona.

"Okay," said Giles. He rose and leaned over and kissed Jewel on her forehead. "I'll see you later, my love." Giles picked up the food and smiled at Manny and Mona as he left.

Mona turned into Manny's arms. They closed around her and he held her while she got her emotions under control. Mona pulled back and gazed up at Manny. "It just strikes me harder sometimes," she confessed.

"I know, but you can always lean on me. I will be here for you," said Manny giving her another hug.

"Thank you," said Mona, hugging him back.

She turned and sat at Jewel's bedside in the chair Giles

LOVE'S PROMISE

had just vacated. Manny pulled another chair up beside her so they could touch.

Mona took her mom's hand. "Manny and I are back, Mom. We sent Giles home to get some rest. We are not going to leave you alone. We will be here until Giles returns. We ran into Arnold Payne downstairs. He was here making a donation for his dad. He is married to Mary Ellen, and they are expecting a baby. I think he and Charise have finally managed to convince their dads to stop interfering in their lives. They are both happier now that they are with their own true loves."

Mona glanced at Manny and smiled back at him when he smiled at her. "I know I am happier now that Manny and I are together. We are meant to be together. I love him, Mom," said Mona with a smile for Manny.

Manny leaned forward and kissed her. "I love you, too," he whispered.

Mona leaned back in her chair and looked at Manny. "I just realized it's only a week until Christmas. I need to go Christmas shopping. I have to buy some Christmas presents. I think it would be best for the presents Mom and Giles have for the kids to wait until Mom gets home, and they can have their Christmas then."

"Good idea," said Manny. "Dad was going to get a tree today. Poppie and Glen can help him, and mom decorate it. We can go shopping after Giles returns."

Mona smiled at Manny. "Are you sure you don't mind taking me shopping?"

"I will be able to get some ideas from you about presents. Do you think we should bring Beth over to the ranch so she will be with family for Christmas?" asked Manny.

"Do you think your mom and dad will be okay with adding one more to our group?" asked Mona.

119

"They will be fine with it. She can share Poppie's room, and I think she will be happier around her family," said Manny.

"Okay, I will talk to Cathy and, if it is okay with her, I'll talk to Beth. Thank you for thinking about it," said Mona.

"I should warn you about my grandfather. He might show up sometimes during Christmas. He stays pretty busy with Sebastian Kantor, and he is not as grouchy as he used to be, but we all try to avoid him when we can," said Manny.

"I met him once when I was a little girl. He came by to talk to Mom about leasing our land. He glowered at me, and I hid behind Mom. After he left, Mom told me not to be afraid. Stand up and face his scowl. She said people like him have more respect for you if they can't make you shiver. I always remembered that advice. Anytime anyone gave me attitude, I stood up straight and stared right back at them and dared them to try anything," said Mona.

Manny laughed. He put an arm around her and kissed her lightly. "My brave warrior," he said. "I'll call you next time my granddad comes around. You can protect me."

"I would," agreed Mona. "Call me anytime. I'll be right there by your side daring him to try anything. Does your granddad live on the ranch?"

"Yes, but he has his own house. He hasn't been there much for a while. I think Sebastian has a hunting cabin and they spend a lot of their time there," said Manny.

"Does your mom do a lot for Christmas?" asked Mona.

"She will try to get as much of the family as she can together for a meal and to exchange presents," said Manny.

"We celebrate more since Katie came home. Before that, we just went through the motions. Our hearts weren't in it. We would eat as fast as we could and find something to do on the ranch. After David and Lee married, they started their own traditions and didn't come over, hardly at all. They have just started bringing the girls over and letting them visit. I hope Granddad doesn't spoil it for Mom," said Manny with a sigh.

Mona patted him on the arm. "Don't worry, you have me now. Everything is going to be alright," said Mona.

Manny smiled and squeezed her hand. "I am blessed to have you in my corner," said Manny.

"You will have to help me make a list of everyone I need to get gifts for and maybe give me some ideas of what they like," said Mona.

"You don't have to get gifts for everyone," protested Manny.

"Well, at least the girls. If I am going to be their favorite aunt, I have to get them a Christmas present," said Mona.

"Well, the girls are into riding. They have their own ponies. Katie bought them grooming kits last year," said Manny.

Mona smiled up at Manny. "I know it is a shame when I am in love with a guy who raises horses, but I don't know very much about horses. Glen probably knows more than I do," said Mona.

"We'll go to the western store and see what we can find," said Manny. "I was thinking about getting Glen a western hat."

"He would love a real cowboy hat," said Mona. "Maybe I could get him a western shirt with fringe on it to go with the hat."

"What about Beth and Poppie?" asked Manny.

"Why don't we get them hats and shirts, too? If they are going to be spending any time on the ranch, they will need the hats to protect them from the sun," said Mona.

"Okay, we have them taken care of, maybe this shopping won't be so bad," said Manny.

Mona laughed. "We are just getting started," she said.

Manny groaned.

"If you don't want to go with me, I can go by myself," said Mona.

Manny tightened his arm around her. "Not a chance. I am not letting you out of my sight until I put a ring on your finger, and probably not then either," said Manny.

Mona leaned in and kissed him. "I know just how you feel. I can hardly stand to not be close to you. I feel like a part of me is missing when you are not there with me," she said.

Manny pulled her into his lap, and she leaned her head on his shoulder. Mona kissed him softly.

"I agree," said Manny. "We are going to have to wait until after your mom's operation to do most of our Christmas shopping."

"I know," said Mona. "I was just trying to distract myself."

"What do you want for Christmas?" asked Mona.

"You" Manny reached into his pocket and pulled out a ring box. He opened it and showed the ring to Mona. "This was my Grandma Sybil's ring. She gave it to me and told me to keep it for a special lady. I will never find anyone more special than you," said Manny.

Mona gazed at the ring. It had an opal surrounded by diamonds on a white gold band. "It is absolutely beautiful," said Mona. "I will be honored to wear it."

Manny took her hand and slid the ring on her finger. It fit like it had been made for her. Mona held up her hand and admired the ring.

"I love it," she said, kissing Manny again. "I promise I will treasure it, and someday maybe we can pass it down to a son of our own."

They both looked up when the door opened and the doctor entered. He had another doctor with him, and they both rose to greet the doctors.

"Miss Santoes, Mr. McCray, this is Doctor Marks. He will be performing Mrs. Santoes' operation," said the doctor.

"It is nice to meet you, Doctor Marks," said Mona.

Manny shook his hand, and the doctors turned to Jewel.

They checked the charts and looked over the information. When they turned to leave, Dr. Marks looked at Mona. "I have studied the x-rays and all of the tests. We should be able to remove the tumor with no problem. After the operation, we will keep Mrs. Santoes in a coma for a few days to give her brain a chance to get over the trauma. If we wake her up too soon, it will put more stress on her body."

"So, she won't be awakened for a few days," said Mona.

"No, I wanted you to understand. Not waking up is not going to be a bad sign. It will be a part of the process of making her better," said Dr. Marks.

"I see," said Mona. "Thank you for telling me. I'll pass the information on to my stepdad."

"The operation will be early in the morning. It is a delicate operation, and it will take about four hours. I want to be fresh starting out," said Dr. Marks.

Mona nodded. "Get some rest, Doctor," she said.

Manny had kept his arm around her to lend her strength while she talked to the doctor. He nodded to both doctors as they nodded before leaving.

When they were gone, Mona took a deep breath. She looked up at Manny. "It's really going to happen. I'm scared, Manny," she said and buried her face in his chest.

"I know you are," said Manny, holding her close. "I'm here. I'll be with you all the way. Should we call Giles?"

Mona looked at the time. "There's nothing he can do. Let

him sleep a little longer. He is going to need it to get through tomorrow."

"Yes, it's going to be a long day," agreed Manny.

Manny sat down and pulled her down onto his lap so he could hold her close and comfort her. They sat quietly thinking about the future and the trials ahead of them. Sometimes it seemed as if they would always be striving to fulfill love's promise for the future.

Mona sighed as she said a silent prayer for her mom's recovery. Manny held her close as he said his own prayer.

CHAPTER 14

*G*iles came back early. He had a few hours of sleep, but Mona was hoping he would get more. They explained to him about the doctor coming by and telling them about the early morning surgery.

"We are going to see if Beth wants to join Poppie and Glen at the ranch. We thought she would be better if she is with them," explained Manny.

Giles nodded. "I have been worried about her. She acts tough, but she is very sensitive," he said.

Mona looked at Giles in surprise. She had never thought of Beth as being sensitive. She had always seemed to be running things with Poppie and Glen. Sensitive was not a word she would have applied to Beth.

"Manny and I are going to do a little Christmas shopping. We thought we should leave the kids presents and let them have Christmas with Mom when she comes home," said Mona.

"Okay, whatever you think best," agreed Giles. "I know Jewel loves Christmas." They left to go shopping, and Giles sat down in the chair beside Jewel's bed and took her hand.

Mona and Manny stopped by the western store in Sharpville. It was larger and had a better selection than the one in Barons. After looking around for a while, Manny decided they needed boots to go with the hats. "These boots go perfect with the hat I picked out for Glen," said Manny.

Mona grinned. Manny was really getting into his shopping. She picked out a shirt to go with Glen's new boots and hat. They put them in the buggy and started looking for hats and boots for the girls. Manny wasn't as picky over the girls' outfits, so they quickly finished their shopping. Mona found a shirt she added for Alvin, and an apron she spotted with "Cathy" written across the front was added for Cathy. She had been keeping an eye out for something for Manny, but she hadn't seen anything she liked. They paid for their purchases and put them in the trunk of the car. They were going to stop by and see if Beth wanted to come with them, and they didn't want her to see the gifts.

Beth was delighted to be going with them and went to gather her things while Mona thanked Sharon for having Beth stay with her. Mona had called Cathy while they were waiting at the hospital and asked her if it was okay for Beth to join Poppie and Glen. Cathy said she was more than welcome. Mona got misty-eyed when she thought what a wonderful mother-in-law she was getting.

While Mona took Beth in and introduced her to Cathy and Alvin, Manny slipped their presents up to Mona's room so they could wrap them later. He threw a blanket over them, just in case someone came into the room before they could get them wrapped.

When he returned to the living room, he found Glen and Poppie excitedly filling Beth in on life on the ranch and all they had been doing. Beth sat wide-eyed listening. She looked wistful, like she was sorry she had been missing out on a lot of fun.

Mona smiled at her and told Poppie to show Beth the room they would be sharing. The girls obediently took Beth's bag and headed for Poppie's room.

Manny went to the kitchen and asked Cathy for some wrapping paper, tape, and bows. She gathered the items for him, and he collected Mona, and they went to wrap presents. Mona turned the lock on her door so no one would come in and see the presents before they could get them wrapped. They had noticed the Christmas tree in the living room when they came in. Alvin and the kids were not finished decorating it yet.

They took the presents down and put them under the unfinished tree when they were through wrapping them. There would soon be more presents joining them. Mona had not found anything for David's girls yet. She couldn't decide what to get two little girls who were horse crazy and she hadn't met them yet. It was hard to think of what someone would like if you didn't know them.

Getting something for Manny was also a problem. Nothing seemed just right. Mona sighed and decided to put the problem aside. She wouldn't be doing any more shopping until after her mom's operation.

The kids settled in the living room to talk and catch Beth up on all the news. Manny and Alvin went out to the barn so Alvin could catch Manny up on ranch business. Cathy and Mona went into the kitchen to plan a special Christmas dinner menu.

"I talked to Katie. She and Carlos are coming. Star and Sam will be here, and I finally managed to get David and Lee to agree to come by after the girls get their Santa gifts," said Cathy.

"You are going to have a house full," said Mona.

Cathy smiled. "Yes, it will be great. The only thing better would be if Thomas could be here, also," said Cathy.

"Have you talked to him?" asked Mona.

"Yes, he said he was waiting for orders. He didn't think they were going to get leave," said Cathy.

"That's too bad," said Mona.

Cathy shook her head. "I miss Thomas. He was the youngest at home after Katie was taken to her Aunt's. He and I were close because the older boys spent most of their time out on the ranch. He worked on the ranch also, but Alvin tried to leave him with me as much as he could, so I wouldn't be alone. He wanted someone here who could let him know if his dad started any trouble," said Cathy.

"Did his dad start any trouble?" asked Mona.

"Yes, he tried, but Alvin stopped him. He told him he would send him to the hospital and to jail if he didn't leave me alone. Amos wasn't physical with his abuse. He was a bully, but it was mostly verbal. I am so glad he and Sebastian Kantor made up. It is so much more peaceful without him around," said Cathy.

Mona grinned. "It sounds like it is much better. I hope he doesn't come around before Mom gets out of the hospital. Poppie, Beth, and Glen do not need to deal with him on top of everything else," said Mona.

"I don't think you have to worry. If he does come by, he will probably just ignore them. He doesn't know who they are," said Cathy.

"I was wondering if you had any ideas about what Manny would like for Christmas. I can't seem to find anything suitable," said Mona.

"I don't know. He is very quiet about what he likes," said Cathy with a smile. "I think if you ask him, he will say he has everything he could possibly want. He is very hard to shop for. After your mom is over her operation, we can leave the kids with Manny and Alvin and go Christmas shopping, just the two of us," said Cathy.

"I would like that," agreed Mona.

Manny and Alvin came in the back door. Alvin went to Cathy to give her a kiss, and Manny headed for Mona for his own kiss.

Mona kissed him back and tugged his hand, so he sat in the chair next to her. Manny put his arm around her and kissed her again. Mona raised her hand to caress his face.

"Oh," said Cathy. "You gave Mona Grandma Sybil's ring," said Cathy with a smile.

Mona held her hand up and smiled. "Yes, it is beautiful," said Mona.

"I always thought so," said Cathy. "You do know she inherited the ring from her mother. Amos didn't give it to her," said Cathy.

"I'm glad," said Mona. "It makes it even more special."

"I knew it was from her mother," said Manny. "She told me when she gave it to me."

Cathy got up and came around the table and hugged both of them. "Congratulations. I know you were already engaged, but this makes it more official," said Cathy.

Alvin came around behind Cathy. "Welcome to our family, Mona. I am glad you are wearing my mom's ring. I was always fond of it," said Alvin.

"I promise, I'll take very good care of it and someday pass it down to one of your grandchildren," said Mona.

Alvin looked at Manny and smiled. "She's a keeper," he said.

Mona flushed with pleasure and Manny smiled down at her and kissed her again. "Yes, she is," he agreed.

"Why don't we order some pizzas from Barons?" asked Manny. "The kids would love it and it will give Mom a break in the kitchen."

"Okay," agreed Alvin. "I know you two will be up very early to be there for the operation. Do you know what time it will be?"

"No, I just know it will be early. They will have to get Mom ready. They have to shave her head. Mom's going to hate that," said Mona.

"Her hair will grow back. While she is waiting, she can wear a wig. Just think she can experiment with different colors and see which suits her best. The Cut and Curl should have some in stock," said Cathy.

"Yes, they do," agreed Mona with a smile. "Mom was always talking about trying different colors. Now, she can. I can even get Pat to give me a discount on them."

Manny took out his phone to order the pizzas. "Is there anything you don't want on your pizza?" he asked.

Mona shook her head. "As long as it is on pizza, everything is fine. Order what you like," she said.

Manny ordered four large supreme pizzas. "They will be here in about forty-five minutes," he said.

Glen came into the room and stood next to Manny. Manny reached out an arm and gave him a hug. "Are you tired of girl talk?" asked Manny.

Glen flushed slightly. "All they want to talk about is how cute some boy at school is," said Glen with a disgusted look. The adults all laughed softly.

"It is a girl thing," said Mona. "In a few years, you will be glad when some girl thinks you are cute."

"They already think I am cute," said Glen. "They just don't talk about it all the time."

"Well," laughed Mona. "My little Casanova, we will have to keep an eye on you."

Everyone laughed again. Glen just looked confused. "Could I have something to drink?" asked Glen.

"Sure," said Cathy. "Get a Kool-Aid pouch. Take one to your sisters, too. We have pizza coming, so we will eat soon."

"Alright," said Glen as he took three packets out of the refrigerator and headed to the living room to give two of them to Beth and Poppie. He also wanted to inform them about the expected pizza.

Mona shook her head. "They can sure surprise you," she said. "You never know what to expect."

"They keep life interesting," agreed Alvin. "They keep us on our toes and sometimes make us feel young; other times, they can make you feel very old."

Cathy squeezed his arm. "Life always shows us the unexpected. As long as you can see the beauty in life, you will never be old at heart," she said.

Alvin smiled at Cathy. "I am blessed to have you by my side to remind me to look for the beauty in life, but my most important blessing is right here by my side," he said, kissing her.

Manny smiled. He was so happy to see his parents so much in love. They had the kind of relationship he wanted for him and Mona. When he looked into her misty eyes, he knew she agreed with him. Mona smiled at Manny and raised her lips for a kiss.

They all enjoyed the pizza, and then Manny and Mona went to try and get some sleep. They said good night at Mona's door with a kiss. Mona went into her room, and Manny went to his room. They both went to sleep without trying to mind talk. They knew there was a stressful day ahead of them.

Mona and Manny arrived at the hospital early. No one had been up when they left, but they found the nurses were already preparing Jewel for surgery. They found Giles in the hall outside Jewel's room. The nurses had asked him to leave while they prepared her for surgery. Mona gave him a hug and Manny patted him on the back.

Giles smiled mistily at them. "It's hard to trust these people with my life," he said. "Jewel is my life."

"We know," said Manny. Mona nodded and looked away to hide her own tears. Manny hugged her, and she turned her face to his chest.

The nurses came out and told them they could go in for a little while until they came to take Jewel down for surgery. They went inside and found Jewel face down in a special pillow. It had a round hole in it where her face fit. Her hair was all gone, and she was dressed in a gown for surgery.

Giles went over to her side and took her hand. "You come back to me," he said. "We have a lot of living to do. I'm not ready to be alone. I need you, and the kids need you. You fight to stay with us where you belong."

He had barely finished talking when the orderlies came in to take her down to surgery.

"There is a waiting room next to surgery where you can wait, and there is a chapel close by," said one of the orderlies.

"Thank you," said Mona as they followed the bed with Jewel on it down the hall. When the bed was rolled into the elevator, they watched the doors close and waited for the next one so they could go down to the surgical waiting room.

Several nurses passed by and wished them good luck while they were waiting. Mona and Manny smiled and thanked them, but Giles just stared like he was in a trance.

When they reached the surgical floor, they went down to the waiting room. Giles stopped before entering. He was looking at the sign for the chapel. "I'll be back in a little while. If you need me, I'll be in the chapel," he said. He turned and headed for the chapel.

"Do you think we should go with him?" asked Mona.

Manny shook his head. "I think he wants to be alone. There may be a preacher in there to talk to him," he said. Mona gazed after Giles for a minute before turning and going into the waiting room. There was no one there. It was very early. The room would probably fill up later as other doctors had patients brought in for surgery.

Mona headed for a sofa so she and Manny could sit beside each other. Mona glanced at her watch. The doctor had said the surgery on her mom would last about four hours, but it probably hadn't started yet.

They had been sitting there for about thirty minutes when a nurse stuck her head in the door told them surgery was starting. Mona looked at her watch again and held tightly to Manny's hand.

"Do you think we should go and tell Giles?" she asked.

Manny shook his head. "We can tell him when he comes back. There is nothing he can do here but worry. Maybe the chapel can help him have more hope," said Manny.

Mona nodded. She took out her phone and called Pat at the Cut and Curl.

"Hello, Mona, how is Jewel doing?" asked Pat.

"She is in surgery. They had to shave her head. I was wondering if you could put aside several wigs for her to use while her hair is growing back?" asked Mona.

"Sure, I'll go and pick some out and put them in my office so they don't get used. I should have thought of it before," said Pat. "Let me know as soon as there is any news."

"Thanks, Pat. I'll let you know," said Mona as she hung up.

Mona looked at Manny. "I know it could have waited. It was something to do. I wish there was something else I could do. This waiting is awful."

"I know. Call anybody you want to. It won't hurt anything, and maybe it can ease your mind for a minute or two," said Manny.

Mona leaned over and kissed him. "You are an amazing man. I wish there was something I could do for the magic mirror to thank it for bringing you to my attention."

"As long as we are fulfilling the promise of love the mirror gave to us, we are thanking the magic mirror. Maybe it will keep bringing true love into the lives of deserving couples," said Manny.

When Mona looked at her watch again, she and Manny had been sitting and talking for almost two hours. Other people had come gone, but they had the room to themselves again.

A nurse stuck her head into the room and told them everything was going well. They smiled and thanked her.

Giles had not returned to the waiting room. Mona hoped he had someone with him to counsel him. They were about halfway through. Manny had called Cathy and updated her and Alvin. They told him to keep in touch.

The four hours were about up when Giles came through the waiting room door. He looked much better as he looked at them for information.

"The nurse told us everything was going well about two hours ago," said Mona.

Giles nodded and came over and sat down. He had barely seated himself when the door opened and both doctors came in. They were smiling. "Is she alright?" asked Giles.

"The surgery went fine. We got the entire tumor. She will be in recovery for a while until the anesthesia wears off. She will be in a coma for a few more days, but as soon as she is out of recovery, she will be taken back to her room and you can be with her. I am going to stick around for a day to keep an eye on her, but I don't think we have anything to worry about." said the surgeon.

"Giles went over and shook his hand. "Thank you, Doctor," he said.

"Give us another thirty minutes, and you can see her," he said.

Giles nodded and thanked him again. The doctors left. Giles, Mona, and Manny went up to the floor where Jewel's room was and went to the waiting room to wait for her return.

Mona blinked back tears, and Manny held her close. Mona looked up at Manny and smiled. "My mom is going to be alright," she whispered. Manny nodded and held her tight.

Giles smiled at them both.

CHAPTER 15

The next two days were less stressful. They had put a cot in Jewel's room so Giles could stay with her and still get some sleep. Since they were assured of Jewel's recovery, there was a more relaxed air in her room. She was still lying face down on the special pillow so she would not hurt her head where she was operated on.

Mona and Manny were not spending as much time at the hospital. They would go by and see how everything was and then leave. Manny was helping out more on the ranch, and Mona was helping Cathy get ready for Christmas.

Mona and Cathy cornered Manny and Alvin and asked them to watch the kids the next day while they went shopping. There was only four days, counting today, until Christmas, and they both had a lot of shopping left to do. Mona wanted to get Manny a Christmas present. She had an idea, but she had to see if she could pull it off. To do it, she had to talk to her friend Nessie without Manny around. She wanted Cathy around to help her arrange his surprise.

Manny and Alvin agreed to watch the kids, and Mona was supper excited. She could hardly wait for the next day.

She and Cathy had talked about presents for David and Lee's girls. Cathy suggested Western shirts with a more feminine look. She said the shirts they had were too masculine. The girls were growing up to be tomboys and Cathy wanted them to be reminded they were girls. Mona liked her idea and decided to see if she could find shirts like Cathy described.

Mona had drawn a picture of the magic mirror. She used a program on her computer to add pictures of Katie and Carlos, Sam and Star, her and Manny, Joey and Hallie, Charise and Zachery. They were all gathered around the magic mirror. She made copies of her design and bought frames for them. She made six copies. She was giving one to Katie and Carlos for Christmas. She had one for Sam and Star. She wrapped it up and put it under the tree. She had one for Alvin and Cathy. She put theirs under the tree, also. The one for her and Manny, she put under the tree with Manny's name on it. The pictures for Joey and Hallie, and Charise and Zachery she wrapped up and saved them to deliver later. Mona was very pleased with how well the pictures had turned out.

Mona had called her friend Nessie. Nessie worked at the courthouse, and Mona was checking to be sure if she was going to be at work the next day. Mona explained what she wanted to do, and Nessie was very excited to help her. Nessie told Mona to come by about lunchtime and she could fill out the papers while her assistant was gone to lunch.

The next morning, Cathy and Mona kissed their guys goodbye and very excitedly started on their shopping trip. While they were on their way to town, Mona decided she needed to tell Cathy what she was up to.

"Cathy, I told you I was trying to think of something special for Manny for Christmas. Well, I think I may have come up with something special," said Mona.

Cathy smiled. She could see how excited Mona was. "What did you come up with?" she asked.

"Well, when I asked Manny what he wanted for Christmas, he said he wanted me and proposed. Well, I talked to my friend Nessie. She works at the courthouse, and she prepares marriage licenses. If I go by and fill out the paperwork, Nessie can bring the license by the ranch on Christmas day. She is a notary, and after Manny and I sign it, we can be married, and she can notarize it and file it for us. I was hoping you could talk to the preacher and see if he could come over long enough to marry us."

Mona looked up at Cathy. Cathy smiled. "We are almost at the church. Let's stop and ask him," she said.

Cathy pulled into the parking lot at the church. They got out and went next door to the preacher's house. His wife came to the door, and Cathy smiled and asked her if her husband was home. She invited them in and went to fetch her husband.

"Hello, Cathy," said the preacher. "What can I do for you?" he asked.

"This is my son Manny's fiancée. We were wondering if you could spare a short time on Christmas day to perform a wedding ceremony for her and Manny. Mona doesn't want anyone to know about it. She wants to surprise Manny."

"He has to be agreeable. I can't do a wedding if either of the participants is not agreeable," he said.

"He is agreeable. We have had to delay getting married because my mom was in the hospital," said Mona.

"How is your mom?" asked the preacher.

"She is better. We will probably have another ceremony when she can attend," said Mona.

"What time would you want me to be there?" he asked.

Mona looked at Cathy. "How about eleven?" Cathy asked.

"Okay, I'll be there at ten-thirty so I can talk to Manny first," said the preacher.

The ladies stood up smiling. "Thank you, we will see you then," said Cathy.

"Yes, thank you," said Mona.

The ladies hurried on to town. They had a lot of shopping to do. Cathy insisted Mona needed a new dress. They went by the western store first and found shirts for David's girls. Cathy bought them some new small-size lassos. They stopped at the dress store, and Mona found a dress.

"You know I could have worn the dress I wore at Charise and Zachery's wedding," said Mona.

"No, you needed something Manny hasn't seen before," said Cathy.

They picked up a few more gifts for Cathy to pass out and then headed for the courthouse.

They went in and Nessie smiled at them.

"Cathy, this is my friend Nessie Bromen. Nessie, this is Manny's mom, Cathy McCray," said Mona.

"It's nice to meet you, Mrs. McCray. I've known Manny a long time. He is a nice guy," said Nessie.

"Thank you," said Cathy. "It's always nice to hear good things about my sons."

Nessie smiled and pulled out the forms. "If you two will fill out these, I'll check them over," said Nessie.

"I'll fill out my information, and you can do Manny's," said Mona.

Mona filled out her information and then gave the form to Cathy. Cathy filled out Manny's information, and they handed the form back to Nessie. Nessie looked over the form and smiled. "It's all in order. All I have to do is have you and

Manny sign it along with the preacher and two witnesses. I'll notarize it and then I'll bring it in and file it at it at the court-house the day after Christmas. What time do you want me to be at the ranch?" asked Nessie.

"Ten-thirty Christmas morning," said Mona.

"Okay, I'll be there," said Nessie.

"Thanks, I really appreciate your help," said Mona.

Nessie grinned. "We magic mirror girls have to stick together. If you hear anything about Dawson arriving before I do, let me know."

"I'll do that," agreed Mona. "We will see you at Christmas."

Mona and Cathy left to finish shopping. They went to the grocery store and Cathy stocked up on some things. One good thing about having a smokehouse was they didn't have to buy any meat.

After they finished at the grocery, they headed home. Mona took out her phone and called Giles. She explained what she was doing and assured him they would have another ceremony when Jewel could attend,

"Could you come out to the ranch long enough to give me away and wish Poppie, Beth, and Glen Merry Christmas?" asked Mona.

"If your mom is okay, I'll come," said Giles. "I am glad you and Manny are going ahead and not waiting. Love should never be put on hold," said Giles.

"Thanks," said Mona. After she hung up, she looked at Cathy.

"He said he was glad we were not waiting. He said love should never be put on hold," said Mona.

"He sounds like a very nice man," said Cathy.

"Yes, he is," agreed Mona.

They pulled into the ranch, and everyone piled out to

help carry in the packages. Mona followed them into the kitchen and separated her packages. She took them upstairs before anyone saw her dress. She hung up her dress and wrapped the shirts for the girls. She took the presents down and put them under the tree. There was beginning to be a large stack of gifts under the tree. Everyone kept adding things under it. Alvin and the kids had finished decorating it, and it looked great. Mona stood back and gazed up at it. Manny came up behind her and put his arms around her and held her close.

"I missed you," he said.

"I wasn't gone long," said Mona.

"I have gotten used to being with you. I can see right now I will have to work close to home so I can pop in and hold you often," said Manny.

"I am all for having you close," said Mona turning and kissing him.

Glen came into the room. He smiled when he saw Mona and Manny kissing.

Mona glanced at him. "Why are you smiling?" she asked.

"I am just so happy you are marrying Manny," said Glen.

"I am glad you approve," said Mona.

"Dad and I won't be the only boys anymore," he said.

Mona and Manny laughed. "Well, at least he approves," said Manny.

"Yes," said Mona. "I need to go and help Cathy with supper."

She kissed him one more time and headed for the kitchen. She was so excited. In just three days, she would be Mrs. Manuel McCray.

She walked into the kitchen like she was floating on air.

The next morning after Manny and Alvin had gone out to work, Amos McCray came to the ranch house. Glen opened the door for him and stood looking at him, waiting for him to say what he wanted. Glen did not know who he was.

Amos smiled. "Who are you, young man?" he asked.

"I'm Glen Santoes. Who are you?" asked Glen.

"I'm Amos McCray," Amos replied.

"Oh, you're Manny's mean granddad," said Glen.

Amos laughed. "Yes, I suppose I am," he replied.

Cathy heard Amos talking and came in from the kitchen. "Amos," she said. "Alvin and Manny are out at the barn. I suppose they will be in soon for breakfast. Come in."

Amos came in and looked at Glen. "I heard about your mom. How is she doing?" Amos asked.

"She is doing better since the operation," replied Glen.

"Good, I'm glad she is doing better. She is a fine woman," said Amos.

"Thank you," said Glen.

"Glen, why don' you go and see if Poppie and Beth are ready for breakfast?" suggested Cathy.

"Yes, Ma'am," said Glen, and he took off upstairs to get his sisters.

Amos turned to Cathy and sighed. "Is their mom really going to be alright?" he asked.

"Yes. Come into the dining room and join us for breakfast," said Cathy.

She turned and led the way to the dining room. Mona was there fixing the plates for the kids. When Cathy came in with Amos following her, Mona smiled.

"We have one more for breakfast," said Cathy.

"Good morning," said Mona as she went to get another plate of food.

"Good morning," said Amos.

"Mona, this is Amos McCray," said Cathy.

Mona nodded. "Yes, I know. I saw him when he talked to my mom about leasing our land."

Amos looked startled. "You were just a little girl, and it was a long time ago. How can you remember me?" asked Amos.

Before he could answer, Alvin and Manny came through the back door. They stopped at seeing Amos there talking calmly to Mona and Cathy.

"Dad," said Alvin. "Is Sebastian here, too?"

"He's waiting in the car," said Amos.

"Manny, go tell Sebastian to come in and eat breakfast," said Cathy. "Wait in the car, indeed," mumbled Cathy.

Alvin and Amos grinned but didn't say anything as Manny left to get Sebastian. Manny entered a few minutes later with Sebastian following him.

"Good morning, Sebastian," said Cathy. "Sit down. Mona will get you a plate."

Sebastian sat down and smiled at Mona as she sat a plate of food in front of him and one in front of Amos. Mona brought plates for Alvin and Manny also. The kids came hurrying in and sat at their plates. Mona had already placed them on the table. Sebastian looked curiously at the children but didn't say anything.

"I came by this morning to give you and Cathy your Christmas present," said Amos between bites.

"We were not expecting a present from you," said Cathy.

"I know. It's not really a Christmas present. It's something I wanted to do," said Amos. He took an envelope out of his pocket and handed it to Alvin.

Alvin opened the envelope and looked inside. He looked up, startled. "Are you sure you want to do this?" asked Alvin.

Amos nodded. "Very sure."

"What is it?" asked Cathy.

"It's a deed to the ranch transferring ownership to me and Cathy," said Alvin. Everyone looked at Amos, astonished.

"All except my house and twenty-five acres," said Amos. "I transferred my place to Manny."

"Why me?" asked Manny.

"Because you stayed here and helped your dad take care of the place. Katie has her shop. Sam has his place, and David has his own place. Your dad can decide how to divide between the others later. I heard you were getting married, and you need your own place," said Amos.

"Thanks," said Manny. He grinned at Mona. She smiled back at him.

"I noticed she was wearing Sybil's ring," said Amos. "Sybil would be very pleased."

"I am glad," said Mona. "We will take good care of your place."

"It's not my place anymore. It's your place," said Amos handing the deed to his house and twenty-five acres to Manny.

Sebastian sat looking at everyone and smiled big.

"Where are you going to live?" asked Glen. Everyone looked at him, and he shrugged. "Well, he is giving away the ranch and his house. I was just wondering where he was going to live," said Glen.

Everyone looked at Amos. He smiled at Glen. "Smart boy," he said. "I have bought Sebastian's hunting cottage. I will live there, so I will be close enough to go fishing anytime we want to."

Sebastian nodded. He was smiling at everyone, very pleased with how things were going.

Alvin shook his head. "I don't know what to say. I never expected this," he said.

Amos and Sebastian finished their food and stood up. "I

know you didn't, but it was time. You have earned it. We have to go. There is a big fish with my name on it," said Amos smiling at Sebastian.

All of the adults followed as they headed for the door. The kids stayed where they were and finished eating. The adults came back inside after watching Amos and Sebastian leave.

Alvin was still looking stunned. Cathy put her arm around him and hugged him tight. "We don't have to worry about him trying to make us leave our home ever again," she said.

Alvin hugged her tight. "Merry Christmas, my love," whispered Alvin."

Manny turned to Mona. "We won't have to build a house. We need to go and look over the house and see what kind of shape it is in," he said.

Manny, holding Mona's hand, started to head for the door, then, he stopped and turned to Alvin. "Do we need to file copies of these at the courthouse?" he asked.

"I don't know," said Alvin taking his deed out and looking at it.

"It says here it has been registered and the courthouse will be sending us a notarized copy in a week or so," said Alvin.

"Okay." Manny started for the door again.

Mona pulled him to a stop. "We need to help clean the kitchen," she protested.

"It's okay," said Cathy. "Go ahead. We will manage."

Mona gave up and followed Manny out. It wasn't far to their new home, but Manny opened the car door for her and drove them the short distance to the house. The house wasn't locked, which was a good thing because Manny had been in such a hurry, he had not stopped for keys.

Manny took her hand and led her to the front door. He

opened the door and stepped inside. Mona looked around. The house was beautiful and very clean. She was sure Cathy had been keeping the house clean. You could see Sybil's influence all through the house as they walked through looking in all of the rooms. A lot of the rooms had covers over the furniture to protect it from dust. It had four bedrooms, two baths, a living room, an office, a den, a washroom, a pantry and front and back porches. The bedrooms had large walk-in closets. Mona sighed. Never had she dreamed she would live in such a beautiful place.

Mona turned and smiled at Manny, who had been watching her face to see her reaction. "It's great. I'm going to love living here with you," she said.

Manny pulled her close and kissed her deeply. "I love you," he said when he had to breathe.

"I love you," said Mona. "Let's go tell the kids about our new home. We can bring them over and let them see it,"

"Okay," agreed Manny.

CHAPTER 16

*A*fter taking the kids to see her new home, Mona called
Nessie and checked to be sure everything was still set
to go for her wedding. Nessie assured her everything was fine.

"Relax, Mona. We have done weddings like this before.
There is nothing improper about it, and all you have to do is
look beautiful," said Nessie.

"I'll do my best," promised Mona. Nessie laughed and
hung up.

Mona asked Cathy for a key to her new home and Cathy
gave her one from the line of keys hanging by the back door.
Cathy helped her gather some sheets and towels and cleaning
supplies. Manny and Alvin had gone to tell David about their
granddad giving them the deeds. They didn't want him to
hear about it from someone else.

Cathy drove Mona and the kids up to the house. She also
brought along some things for the refrigerator. "I doubt you
will be hungry for food at first, but maybe later," she said with
a laugh.

"Thanks," said Mona.

After removing some of the dust covers and cleaning away

any remaining dust, Mona and Beth made the bed in the master bedroom. Poppie took the towels and washcloths and stored them in the master bath.

When Mona started to gather the cleaning supplies to take them back to Cathy's, Cathy told her to leave them there. She had plenty, and Mona would need them until she could buy her own.

The next day was Christmas Eve. The kids were very excited, but Mona was more excited than any of them. Manny looked at her searchingly several times, then he decided maybe she just loved Christmas.

Mona and Cathy were busy making pies and cakes for Christmas. Poppie and Beth helped, but Manny took Glen out to the barn with him, so he would not be by himself.

David had taken the news about the land very well. He had not been expecting anything from Amos, and he was happy for Manny and his parents. He assured them he would bring his family over for Christmas dinner and to open gifts.

The house smelled great with all of the cooking they had been doing. When the guys came in and sniffed and headed for the kitchen, Mona stopped them in their tracks.

"Those desserts are for Christmas. You ask Cathy before you cut anything," she said.

They turned to Cathy and gave her a pleading look. Cathy laughed. "Don't give me your puppy dog look. We will cut one of the pies for supper. Hands off until then."

The guys all turned and headed for the living room. Manny gave Mona a kiss as he passed her on the way to the living room. He followed Alvin and Glen on into the living room where the girls were watching TV. Mona and Cathy laughed at their disappointment. They were soon watching TV with the girls and having a good time debating the show they were watching.

While Christmas Eve went by quickly for everyone else, it seemed to drag for Mona. She had taken some of her and Manny's clothes and put them in the large closet in the master bedroom. She wanted to make sure they had something to change into after they were married.

They all gathered around the tree and sang Christmas carols. After eating popcorn and drinking hot chocolate, they all said goodnight and retired early.

Christmas dawned as a beautiful day. The kids were up and wanting to know when they could open presents.

"We will open them when our guests arrive," said Cathy. She had barley finished talking when Katie and Carlos came in. Star and Sam were right behind them. Katie brought Bambi forward. "I hope you don't mind, I asked Bambi to join us," said Katie.

"It's fine. You are very welcome, Bambi," said Cathy. "Come on in and join the crowd."

"Thank you," said Bambi as she came on in and joined the crowd.

Mona looked at her watch. It was nine o'clock. She pulled Manny aside and told him she needed to talk to him upstairs. He followed her out, and Cathy smiled as she watched them go.

When they got to Mona's room and went inside, Manny drew her into his arms.

"What do you want to talk about?" asked Manny as he nuzzled her neck.

"Do you remember when I asked you what you wanted for Christmas?" asked Mona.

Manny nodded.

"Do you remember what you said?"

"I asked you to marry me," said Manny. He looked at her, wondering where she was headed with these questions.

"Well," said Mona. "I have made arrangements for us to be married this morning," said Mona looking up at him.

Manny looked stunned. "How did you manage to do it?" asked Manny.

"Well, my friend Nessie works at the courthouse. She fills out the marriage license. She is going to bring it out and have us sign it after the preacher marries us. Then, she will notarize it and file it at the courthouse. I talked to Giles, and he is okay with it. I told him we could have another ceremony when Mom is where she can attend. Giles is going to try and be here this morning. The preacher will be here at ten-thirty. The wedding is set for eleven."

Mona paused and looked up at Manny. "You do want to marry me, don't you?"

Manny looked into her face and started smiling. "Yes!!!" he said very loudly. He picked Mona up and swung her around. When he put her down, he took her hand and started for the stairs.

Meanwhile, downstairs, everyone had stopped and looked toward the stairs when Manny shouted.

"What was that?" asked Sam.

"I think Mona just told Manny about his Christmas present," said Cathy with a smile.

No one had a chance to say anything else before Manny came rushing down the stairs with Mona in tow. Manny turned Mona loose and picked up Cathy. He swung her around. "I'm getting married," said Manny as he stood her up straight.

"Yes, I know," said Cathy.

"I am getting married today," said Manny.

"Yes, I know," agreed Cathy calmly.

"Cathy helped me make the arrangements," said Mona with a smile as she took Manny's hand.

"Oh, thanks, Mom," said Manny as he kissed her cheek.

The others were smiling but watching in astonishment. They had never seen Manny act so carefree and happy.

The front door opened, and a man in uniform entered.

"Thomas," exclaimed Cathy as she ran forward to hug her youngest son. Thomas hugged her back and then looked around. "We have quite a crowd," he said.

The door opened again, and David and Lee and the girls entered followed by the preacher.

Cathy led the preacher and Manny into the dining room so they could talk. She had everyone else go into the living room so the adults could start handing out presents to the kids. Mona followed them into the living room. She knew the preacher wanted to talk to Manny alone. She didn't want to put on her dress until she knew the preacher was going to marry them.

David's girls were happy with their shirts and lassos. Glen, Poppie, and Beth were very happy with their western wear. Mona was going to make sure they thanked Manny later. Cathy and Alvin had given Glen a book about horses. They had a cookbook for Poppie. For Beth, they had a dresser set with a brush, comb, and mirror. They all three loved them and hurried over to hug and thank both Alvin and Cathy.

There was a knock at the door, Nessie and Giles came in just as Manny and the preacher came in from the dining room. Everyone was looking toward a grinning Manny.

"It looks like we are going to have a wedding," said the preacher.

Manny came over and hugged Mona. She hugged him back and let out a breath of relief.

"Alright," said Cathy. "Manny, you and Mona go and get changed. You guys help me shift the furniture around so

Manny and Mona can stand over by the tree for the ceremony."

Mona took Nessie's hand and led her upstairs to help her get ready. Thomas followed Manny up to help him. Giles pitched right in and helped move furniture around with Carlos, Sam, and David. The wives stood back and enjoyed seeing their men being bossed around by Cathy. The kids sat back and watched the show.

Alvin led the preacher into the dining room and poured him a glass of iced tea.

It didn't take Manny and Mona long to get ready. When they came back downstairs, they were astonished to see the change in the living room.

They all stood by the Christmas tree, and Cathy gave Katie her camera and told her to take pictures. The preacher asked the normal questions and received the correct responses. Mona was surprised when Manny produced wedding rings for them to exchange. She had not thought about them.

After a long and passionate kiss, Nessie brought forth the license. Manny and Mona and the preacher signed it, Katie and Carlos signed as witnesses. Nessie notarized and stamped it and put it in her purse to record at the courthouse the following day.

Nessie started to leave, but Cathy insisted she stay and eat with them and sample at least one of their desserts. So, Nessie agreed to stay. Cathy encouraged Giles to join them at the table and relax for a while.

When everyone was gone into the dining room, Manny and Mona were still standing by the tree in each other's arms.

"Finally, you are mine," whispered Manny.

"Yes, and you are mine," agreed Mona.

"We are on our way to fulfilling Love's Promise of true love everlasting," said Manny.

"I have our house ready for us. We will be spending the night there," said Mona.

"Oh, yeah," agreed Manny with a smile. He kissed her one more time; then, with her held close to his side, they joined the family for Christmas dinner.

THE END

Dear reader,

We hope you enjoyed reading *Love's Promise*. Please take a moment to leave a review in Amazon, even if it's a short one. Your opinion is important to us.

Discover more books by Betty McLain at https://www.nextchapter.pub/authors/betty-mclain

Want to know when one of our books is free or discounted for Kindle? Join the newsletter at http://eepurl.com/bqqB3H

Best regards,

Betty McLain and the Next Chapter Team

The story continues in:
Love's Voice by Betty McLain

To read the first chapter for free, please head to:
https://www.nextchapter.pub/books/loves-voice

ABOUT THE AUTHOR

With five children, ten grandchildren, and six great-grandchildren, I have a very busy life, but reading and writing have always been a very large and enjoyable part of my life. I have been writing since I was very young. I kept notebooks with my stories in them private. I didn't share them with anyone. They were all handwritten because I was unable to type. We lived in the country, and I had to do most of my writing at night. My days were busy helping with my brothers and sister. I also helped Mom with the garden and canning food for our family. Even though I was tired, I still managed to get my thoughts down on paper at night.

When I married and began raising my family, I continued writing my stories while helping my children through school and into their own lives and families. My sister was the only one to read my stories. She was very encouraging. When my youngest daughter started college, I decided to go to college myself. I had taken my GED at an earlier date and only had to take a class to pass my college entrance tests. I passed with flying colors and even managed to get a partial scholarship. I took computer classes to learn typing. The English and literature classes helped me to polish my stories.

I found public speaking was not for me. I was much more comfortable with the written word, but researching and writing the speeches was helpful. I could use information to build a story. I still managed to put my own spin on the essays.

I finished college with an associate degree and a 3.4 GPA. I had several awards, including President's List, Dean's List, and Faculty List. The school experience helped me gain more confidence in my writing. I want to thank my English teacher in college for giving me more confidence in my writing by telling me that I had a good imagination. She said I told an interesting story. My daughter, who is a very good writer and has books of her own published, convinced me to have some of my stories published. She used her experience self-publishing to publish my stories them for me. The first time I held one of my books in my hands and looked at my name on it as author, I was so proud. They were very well received. This was encouragement enough to convince me to continue writing and publishing. I have been building my library of books written by Betty McLain since then. I also wrote and illustrated several children's books.

Being able to type my stories opened up a whole new world for me. Having access to a computer helped me to look up anything I needed to know and expanded my ability to keep writing my books. Joining Facebook and making friends all over the world expanded my outlook considerably. I was able to understand many different lifestyles and incorporate them in my ideas.

I have heard the saying, "Watch out what you say, and don't make the writer mad, you may end up in a book being eliminated." It is true. All of life is there to stimulate your imagination. It is fun to sit and think about how a thought can be changed to develop a story and to watch the story develop and come alive in your mind. When I get started, the stories almost write themselves; I just have to get all of it down as I think it before it is gone.

I love knowing the stories I have written are being read

and enjoyed by others. It is awe-inspiring to look at the books and think, "I wrote that."

I look forward to many more years of putting my stories out there and hope the people reading my books are looking forward to reading them as much.

Lightning Source UK Ltd.
Milton Keynes UK
UKHW011233091120
373077UK00006B/1074